Cinder-Ugly

by

Laura Strickland

This is a work of fiction. Names, characters, places, and incidents are either the product of the author's imagination or are used fictitiously, and any resemblance to actual persons living or dead, business establishments, events, or locales, is entirely coincidental.

Cinder-Ugly

Contact Information: info@thewildrosepress.com

Cover Art by *Diana Carlile*

The Wild Rose Press, Inc.
PO Box 708
Adams Basin, NY 14410-0708
Visit us at www.thewildrosepress.com

Publishing History
First Fantasy Rose Edition, 2018
Print ISBN 978-1-5092-2165-3
Digital ISBN 978-1-5092-2166-0

Published in the United States of America

I dropped the tray. It fell hard with a clatter that echoed through the room. The remaining tarts—still a generous load—flew everywhere, spewing their jam fillings as they went—on the carpet, on my shoes, on the Queen's skirt, and all over the Prince's sapphire blue legs.

Everything froze. The music paused; everyone stopped talking. Into the resultant silence someone laughed in horror and said, "Oh, my God!"

Mother's face seized in a rictus; she leered at me. For an instant I could see nothing else. Not my father, not Bethessa—who, I'm pretty sure, had laughed—not even the mess that surrounded me like the fallout from an explosion.

Just her anger. Her horror. Her disgust.

Then the moment's paralysis broke. Mother reached out quick as a wasp and slapped me. The blow took me on the cheek, and its force turned my head. Instant tears flooded my eyes.

"Stupid girl!" She drew back her hand to strike again. Two things happened before she could: Father cried, "Erikka—it was my fault!" And the Prince stepped between me and my mother and seized her wrist.

"Please, Madame, do not. It was but an accident."

No rebuke colored his tone. He sounded exceedingly polite. But I knew my mother took it as a rebuke, and a public one. Her face stained with ugly red, and she transferred her glare from me to the Prince.

Even at that moment, that terrible, terrible moment, I knew she would never forgive me for this.

Praise for Cinder-Ugly

"Amazingly emotional, Unique, and fabulously written. I give this 5 stars."

~author and reviewer, Liza O'Connor

~*~

"A magical and very emotional story."

~Petula Winmill

Dedication

To all those who cannot see their own beauty.

Other Books by Laura Strickland
available from The Wild Rose Press, Inc.

Dead Handsome: A Buffalo Steampunk Adventure
Off Kilter: A Buffalo Steampunk Adventure
Sheer Madness: A Buffalo Steampunk Adventure
Steel Kisses: A Buffalo Steampunk Adventure
Last Orders: A Buffalo Steampunk Adventure
~*~
Devil Black
His Wicked Highland Ways
Honor Bound: A Highland Adventure
The White Gull (part of the Lobster Cove Series)
Forged by Love (sequel to *The White Gull*)
Words and Dreams (sequel to *Forged by Love*)
The Hiring Fair (part of the Help Wanted Series)
Awake on Garland Street
Stars in the Morning (part of the Landmarks Series)
Loyal and True
~*~
The Guardians of Sherwood Trilogy:
Daughter of Sherwood
Champion of Sherwood
Lord of Sherwood
~*~
Christmas Short Stories:
Mrs. Claus and the Viking Ship
The Tenth Suitor
Christmastime on Donner's Mountain
~*~
Valentine Short Story:
Ask Me (part of the Candy Hearts Series)

Chapter One

You may think you know my story. But I want to say none of it happened the way you've been told. The facts have been stretched and twisted, braided together the way a maiden's hair is plaited. The story has been shared and shared again so many times the true details are lost. In most instances, the tellers made it the tale they wanted it to be.

If you want the truth, though, I will tell it now—once—while still I can. I am an old woman and not sure how many winters remain to me.

So listen and hear it well.

In those stories told over and over again, they describe me as being relegated to the status of servant by a wicked stepmother who favored her natural daughters over me.

I acted as servant, true, the lowest of the low—the shunned—but that took place in my mother's house. I never had a stepmother; my own blood cast me off. A fiercely elegant woman of high position in our town, Mother enjoyed the prestige of her position and took great pride in her appearance.

And that of her daughters.

She had three daughters in all, I being the youngest, but she would tell you she had only two. She had a fine son also, first born. You never hear about him in any of the stories, but Robin acted kindly toward me, always.

Robin—handsome as my older two sisters were beautiful—stood tall and strongly made. Overtopping our father in height, he had brown hair and grave, dark eyes. You may wonder about my father and why he never interfered in any of the terrible things that occurred. Father, a busy man who served as mayor of our town as well as ran a thriving textile business, could rarely be found at home. Also, wholly besotted with my mother, he tended to let her have her way in all things.

My sisters, Bethessa and Nelissa, followed my mother's lead; I truly can't fault them in anything that occurred. Three and five years my elders respectively, and quite young when I was born, they learned to treat me as they saw me treated, no more.

I have heard many accounts of the morning I was born. Some have been whispered, overheard as gossip, some spoken when the speaker believed I could not hear. Some were even delivered in my mother's dry, matter-of-fact voice. Over the years I have examined, sifted, and distilled them. I can tell you what I believe.

My mother, fully gratified in the three beautiful children she'd already brought into the world, went confidently into delivering me. She had her brown-haired son, then nearly six, and her two golden-headed cherubs. She expected to bear another angel. But things did not go according to plan.

Her first three deliveries had been easy. This one—with me—had her groaning and crying out betimes. A second midwife was called in and, after many hours, a physician. He gave the opinion I would not be born alive.

"Breech, and with a shoulder wedged," he

pronounced, "and likely already dead."

My father was then summoned to make a decision. Should my life—given I still lived—be sacrificed for that of my mother? Or should I be delivered at any cost to her?

I will never understand why my father made the choice he did. He adored his wife and, though proud of his children, he did not believe they compared to her in importance. Nevertheless, he asked the physician to try to deliver me whole—dead or alive.

I was hauled into the world to the sound of my mother's screams—shoulder broken, mewling weakly, ugly and deformed.

I do not believe Mother ever forgave Father for the choice he made. She took it out on me henceforth, and they never had another child. Was that because she never again let him near her in their marriage bed, or because of their mutual horror at what they had produced?

The features that mark me now are in large part the same as those that marked me as an infant. Shoulders too wide, hands too big, head long and domed in back like an egg and covered with mousy brown hair, not hair glossy and shiny with health like Robin's or golden and gleaming like my sisters'. My eyes, like Robin's, were dark. As far as such a thing could be regarded, I took after Father, just as did Robin.

But features that look well enough on a young boy prove less appropriate on a small girl. And mine were exaggerated—the nose and chin too long, the cheekbones askew, one more prominent than the other.

I have often wondered at mother's exact reaction when I issued from her—living after all, yet so hideous.

I have wished to be a fly on that wall, but perhaps it would be entirely too painful to know.

I do know—because I heard our old nurse speak of it much later—that Mother refused to hold me. She declared herself too weak and ill. But she put me from her and never picked me up later, not once.

They had chosen a name for their child should it be a girl—Cindra. And they named me that regardless of my appearance. I recovered from my traumatic birth without my mother's attention and came by my *other* name by the grace of my sister Bethessa, who reportedly said when she first beheld me, "She's not Cindra. She's Cinder-Ugly."

You must understand, I grew up under the blight of my ugliness and never knew anything different. Nurse fed and washed me and rocked my cradle when I cried. She also looked after both my sisters, who regularly had supper with my parents, especially when company came to the house and my mother wished to show them off. No one celebrated my achievements—holding a spoon, sitting up on my own, or taking my first steps. Nurse, kind but busy, made no fuss of me, perhaps believing that if I received little special notice I would not crave it.

In this, though, she erred. My oldest memory is that of wishing not so much for attention as for love. I did not spend a lot of time alone, strictly speaking, since I slept in a little closet off the nursery where my sisters dwelt. But nevertheless, my loneliness went deep.

A child does not recall much before the age of four or five. Even then the memories come in bits and pieces, some of which stand out bright and clear.

I remember my sisters once getting dressed up for some special occasion—a party, I believe it was, there in the house. I must have been about four at the time, which would make them seven and nine. My parents loved to hold dinner parties, but even in my isolation I sensed this as something far grander.

My sisters' excitement testified to it, as did the way Nurse fussed over them with the help of a maid.

I remember Nurse calling them to her so she could inspect them before the maid led them downstairs. Visions they were, and no mistake, one dressed all in pink and one in aqua blue—the very colors delighted my eyes. They shone from their yellow curls, threaded with ribbons, to their polished slippers, and wore identical, self-satisfied expressions.

Looking at them, I began to wail. Nurse had dressed me in my usual brown pinafore that day—brown because it tended to hide dirt—and had not had time to so much as comb my hair. I wanted the pretty colors with a longing that burned at the center of my being, and I reached out to touch the ruffle on the bottom of Nelissa's skirt.

Nurse slapped my hand away, no doubt harder than she intended. I must give Nurse some credit; she was not a particularly cruel woman; she had not the imagination for cruelty, a thing for which my sisters more than compensated.

"No," Nurse snapped, "you will get it dirty."

Nelissa smirked. "She is very dirty, isn't she? Look at her. Dirty as well as ugly. No wonder she has to be hidden away."

I didn't know what "hidden away" meant, not then. I just wanted a pretty dress and ribbons. I started to wail in earnest.

“Be quiet, Cindra,” Nurse told me.

Bethessa laughed. “Yes, be quiet, Cinder-Ugly. You will have your supper here while we get tarts and pies and bonbons.”

Nelissa leaned down to speak into my face. “Bonbons,” she reiterated. “That means ‘good-good,’ because they’re the best thing you’ll never taste.”

Nurse told the maid to take my sisters downstairs. I wept harder, truly inconsolable now, and Nurse, no doubt exhausted and overwrought, turned to me as soon as the door closed behind them.

“Be still, for goodness sake!” she hissed and boxed my ears soundly. “Go play with your cat.”

My cat was not the flesh-and-blood kind. No, though I would have loved that, real cats made Nelissa sneeze. Instead, my “cat” was a shapeless relic that had come to me one Christmas, now so worn with cuddling Nurse had mended it many times.

Still weeping and with my ears burning, I crept off to hold it in my arms and attempt to console myself. I could faintly hear the sounds drifting up from downstairs—music and laughter, excited voices. I knew how the big sitting room looked—I’d been there once or twice. But I couldn’t imagine it full of flowers and candlelight, and people.

I wanted a bonbon—just one—so much it hurt. My sisters could easily have brought me one. But I fell asleep long before they returned to the nursery, and anyway, they never did bring me back treats from any of the parties, not then or later.

Chapter Two

My mother, try as she might, could not keep me hidden in the nursery forever. Eventually we outgrew the nursery, my sisters sooner than I. Despite their myriad petty cruelties, it felt lonely after they migrated to rooms of their own on the floor below, having achieved the status of young ladies. That left just Nurse and me, and the world I could see from the nursery windows.

No one else, except the servants, slept on the top floor of the tall, narrow house. My father being an important man in the town of Salster, the house had many comings and goings, but until I reached eight or so, they meant little to me.

Nobody ever said there was anything wrong with my wits. My sisters had a tutor who taught them, and he also included me in the lessons. I learned to read with lightning speed and soaked up knowledge in a manner that impressed even Master Groat—maybe because I had no distractions. While my sisters worried about properly manicured nails, snags in their silk stockings, and whether their curls fell correctly onto their shoulders, I concentrated on the work itself. In fact, in many ways it saved me.

As soon as I could read, books became treasured companions. I had only a few but didn't hesitate to steal them from the schoolroom. I kept them under the cot where I slept. The characters in those books spoke to me; they were warm, funny, clever, or devious. They taught me how to be.

I must have been eight when, as I say, my parents planned another grand party. From what Nurse said, I gathered they would celebrate an important anniversary—their fifteenth, perhaps, since Robin would have been fourteen by then. I know there was much planning, bustle, and commotion, and I determined I would see it all.

Had I been half as clever as I thought, I'd have realized the truth. Most of the townsfolk must, by then, have forgotten my existence. After all, my mother trotted my brother and sisters out at every available opportunity, but I was never seen. If the family attended an event or function, they went without me. I'd become a detail swept under the rug.

Yet, living in my own head, I forgot that. I merely wanted to see my sisters in their finery—they seldom came up to the nursery anymore. I wanted to behold all the guests arriving in their gilded carriages, and the heaps of food. I wished to hear the music and perhaps dance to it, just once.

But I spent most of my time locked in the nursery. When Nurse went out for any length of time, she took the key with her. On this occasion, with her called to help my sisters dress, I spent most of that day locked in, frustrated and unhappy.

But when Nurse—no longer so young as she had been—returned, she looked exhausted. We ate the cold supper she'd brought—the kitchen had no time to waste on niceties—and put her feet up in her chair, where she soon fell asleep.

She had left the key in the bowl on the table, perhaps never expecting deviousness from me. But I knew an opportunity when I saw one.

When I think now of the pitiful preparations I took, it makes me shudder. I brushed my brown hair carefully and dressed it with plain slides, as I had no ribbons. I could do nothing about my dingy dress or my slippers—my sisters' castoffs. But I borrowed a bobbled shawl left hanging on the back of the door and covered what I could.

Then I peered into the wavy, speckled mirror. Did I look all right? Never having owned any finery, the shawl looked very grand to me. I imagined myself fitting in, slipping between the guests unnoticed, at liberty to listen to the music and sample the food.

I nabbed the key from the bowl and let myself out of the nursery. In the dusty hallway beyond, I stood for a moment breathing deeply, heart racing in my chest. From here, all the sounds intensified—the music flowed up the stairs at me and the laughter tinkled like metal chimes.

I crept down the stairs—the rear stairs, these were, not the grand front set—holding hard to the balustrade. I slid like a shadow through the hallway at the bottom, past the door of the kitchen which heaved with frenetic activity. No one noticed me, and I went on, drawn to the light and beauty like a moth to flame.

Beauty. No one can estimate its importance until deprived of it. I did not mind so much myself being ugly—well, I lie. Perhaps I did mind, but I had at least grown accustomed to it. But I missed color and brightness, even the sight of my sisters in all their finery.

Now I stepped into the grand sitting room, assaulted by it all. A rush of sound, heat, and more color than my senses could quite assimilate.

Guests crowded the room, dancing, laughing, and chattering. Everything glittered, from the jewels they wore to the crystals on the chandeliers. The music seemed to glitter also, to cascade like broken glass.

I paused just inside the doorway as if struck across the face. Whatever I might have imagined while shut away upstairs, this surpassed it. I stood as if rooted, my breath caught in my chest. For several precious moments no one noticed me. Waiters threaded their way among the joyous guests; I might have been invisible.

I could not see my parents anywhere. I think I had some mad notion that I would find them and they would see how well I looked in my borrowed costume and realize how mistaken they'd been in failing to include me all this while.

It didn't happen that way, though. Instead, one of the nearby guests noticed me. He drew his companion's attention to me and they both laughed.

Let me reiterate: for all my other failings, I was not a stupid child. Even though I didn't want to believe it, I knew at that instant that they laughed at and not with me. Their faces jeered at me, and in an effort to get away from them I stumbled farther into the room.

Face after face swiveled toward me. Laugh after laugh sounded. The decibel level in the room seemed to drop till I heard only laughter.

Of the members of my family, Robin saw me first. He hurried over, a look of consternation on his face, and knelt down to take me in his arms.

I still remember how that felt—so seldom was I held by anyone—and how welcome the sense of shelter seemed. But my brother, at fourteen, could in truth do little to shelter me. And next to hurry up, to my everlasting regret, came my mother. She loomed above me and Robin, quite possibly the most sublimely beautiful of all the women present, and began to screech.

"Ah! What is she doing here? Russel! Russel!"

My father, thus summoned, hurried up also. He wore his fancy black suit with the mayor's sash fastened across his chest, and his expression lent me no reassurance. Father had been known to strap Robin and paddle my sisters—though, granted, only for grave offenses.

It came to me I had indeed committed a grave offense.

He and I stared at one another out of almost identical eyes.

"Erikka," he told Mother, "I am sure she merely heard the music and wished to see—"

Mother, in no mood to be appeased, spat at him, "Get her out of here. Where is that nurse, to let her get away? I will strike the woman off!"

I switched my gaze from my father's face to my mother's—flushed dark, it appeared almost purple, and for the first time ever she did not look beautiful. Her emotions had twisted her image into one almost as ugly as mine.

Robin straightened, still holding me in his arms. He pushed my head into his shoulder, exchanged one look with Father, and walked straight from the drawing room.

By the time we got upstairs, I wept with disappointment, with fear, and with the creeping humiliation that on some level always accompanied me. Robin roused Nurse, who swatted me soundly for my escape. Father soon followed and spoke to Nurse in a fierce, low tone, some of which I overheard.

"You are to keep the door locked, especially when we are entertaining."

"Master, I did keep the door locked. She must have got hold of the key, the imp! She grows ever so devious and disobedient with age."

"Nevertheless, she is your responsibility. If you can no longer handle it, we will find someone who can."

Nurse, dismissed? Huddled on my bed where Robin had placed me, I shuddered. I might not love Nurse, nor she me. But she was all I knew—a large part of my narrow world. She might be replaced by someone who would beat me daily instead of delivering the occasional swat.

Nurse said, "She needs a good talking to, that's all. Leave it with me."

Father and Robin left, and Nurse did speak to me, all the while she strapped me with a leather belt across the backs of my legs.

"Something for you to remember," she declared before she left me, taking the key with her.

All that might have been bad enough, but my mother arrived sometime later, near dawn, after the party had ended. Still dressed in her finery, she pounded on the door and woke us both. Nurse let her in.

Mother raged up and down the room. She railed and berated Nurse, spewing words like venom. I do not remember all she said, but her message sounded loud and clear. She did not wish to see me—not ever, if she could manage it. Never while entertaining. By the time she left sometime later, I had indeed learned one important lesson:

My mother was not always beautiful.

Chapter Three

Mother and Father argued about it the next day. I heard bits and pieces of the quarrel because it became very loud and spilled into the front hall. Words floated all the way up the stairs to my ears.

My parents did quarrel sometimes, if Father objected to one of Mother's demands as too outrageous or expensive. She would storm and weep, and he inevitably gave in. This seemed different. It hushed the house, which is what allowed me to hear so much.

The truth is, I did not hear the beginning, which must have taken place in the sitting room. Only when it spilled into the hallway could I hear.

"Erikka, you cannot keep her hidden away forever. Last night proves that. It is not fair, for one thing."

"Not fair? To whom?" Mother wailed.

"To the child."

The child. Even while he defended me, Father would not call me by name.

I stole a look at Nurse, who also listened while trying hard to appear as if she didn't.

"Get away from that door," she snapped at me. "Or do you want another strapping?"

I did not; the welts on my legs already made it hard to stand. I crept away, but both my parents now seemed impassioned. We could still hear almost everything.

"What about being fair to me?" Mother cried,

perhaps predictably. “I have three beautiful children—”

“Four. You have four, Erikka.”

“I have three *beautiful* children! All the world knows them. They’ve forgotten *she* exits. I will *not* remind them.”

“You intend to keep her locked away forever?”

“She is safe. Looked after.”

“She is eight years old. It is no life for her.”

“You do not care about me! You have never cared.”

“That is not true. But to keep a child locked away, lifelong, is a sin. What about when we are gone, tell me that? What will happen to her then?”

“Her sisters will look after her.”

Oh, God help me!

“Her sisters will marry and perhaps move away.”

“Her brother, then. Or…let’s do this, Russel—let’s make provision for her elsewhere. That’s it—we’ll send her away. To a convent, perhaps.”

“You are mad.”

“You know it’s the right thing to do. See to it, Russel.”

The quarrel ended then, though its ramifications remained with me. My sisters soon arrived and taunted me with the information I’d already heard, that I would be sent away. For days after, I waited for the blow to fall, certain I would be banished into an unimagined, outer darkness.

But Father surprised us all. For the first time in memory, he stood up to Mother. One day, in the middle of the afternoon, he came to the nursery and informed Nurse I was to be brought down for dinner.

I will remember that particular meal till my dying

day, every detail of it. Nurse decked me out in one of Nelissa's cast-off dresses and combed my hair into a semblance of order. The fact that it still hung limp and mousy helped nothing. She scrubbed my hands, swiped at my worn shoes, and trotted me downstairs at the appointed hour.

My parents sat at either end of the big, polished table—a place where I'd never before been seated. Granted the seat next to Robin, I found myself opposite my sisters, who shot me sly and disparaging looks, their noses in the air as if they smelled something unpleasant.

After one horrified look at me, Mother turned her eyes away and did not so much as glance at me again. Obviously in high dudgeon, she refused every platter the maids presented to her, which made it impossible for me to eat, in turn.

Father attempted to make conversation. He asked me about my lessons. I answered in mumbles, and my sisters promptly took over the discussion, bragging about a party to which they'd been invited. Only the most elevated of their friends would be there—anyone, basically, worthy of existence.

I do not think I did anything wrong during that meal. I minded my manners, used the proper fork—Nurse had taught me that much—and failed to spill anything. Yet before the pudding made an appearance Mother arose, threw down her napkin, and swept out.

She could not stand to be in the same room with me.

Perhaps Father reached the same conclusion, for his next effort placed me in the kitchen—a room Mother most certainly never visited. Perhaps he considered it a compromise on his part—I could get out of the nursery, yet Mother would not have to see me.

And in the kitchen I stayed for the better part of the next ten years, till the heart of this story begins.

In essence, I suppose, I became a servant in my own home. I graduated from the nursery to one of the narrow rooms on the third floor such as the maids inhabited. Nurse retired and lived in the nursery, nominally still in charge of me.

I spent my days in the kitchen scrubbing vegetables, preparing fish, and sweeping the hearth. Those who came and went in that domain more or less accepted me. New arrivals probably did not know me for a member of the family. Cook treated me neither kindly nor otherwise; after the first year or two, she assigned me chores like everyone else. If I performed them well, she refrained from striking me, for which I felt grateful.

Rarely did I see the other members of my family. My sisters came into the kitchen sometimes to cadge tarts or pastries and lord it over me, boasting about their wardrobes and their conquests.

But I knew most of what went on and lived vicariously through the members of the household. Gossip ran rife in the kitchen, and I had leave to listen to it.

Robin, seldom at home, had joined my father in business. He reportedly courted a young belle to whom he might soon be expected to propose.

My sisters had plenty of beaus and, as might be anticipated, played them off against one another. Neither had as yet accepted any of their numerous proposals. For rumor also had it the Prince—whose castle stood at the top of the hill like the town's crowning jewel—meant at last to take a wife.

Mother had ambitions for her daughters. Lord knew they had ambitions for themselves. The Prince, whose name was Rupert, had been away many years touring the continent, and as a consequence remained largely an unknown quantity. Townsfolk remembered him as a dutiful boy—a handsome, dutiful boy. My sisters focused much on his appearance. But he'd taken his education elsewhere, completing it by seeing the world.

Rumor also had it the kingdom now faced the very real possibility of war with the neighboring realm of Cardonay. My sisters, of course, cared nothing for this. But tradesmen sometimes mentioned it to Cook in passing, citing present uncertainties for the scarcity of the goods she'd ordered. They said Prince Rupert had returned to help his father the King—who failed in his health—prepare for war.

I will admit such a possibility seemed very vague and far away to me. The world itself seemed vague and distant. I'd not been farther out of the house than the garden in many years. What did the affairs of the King mean to me?

I did, though, once hear Father and Robin discussing the possibility of a war. They were in the front parlor, having just entertained a number of other businessmen, and I entered the room to collect glassware and remove the dainties that had been put out. Deep in discussion, neither of them paid me any heed.

"—do you think will come of it?" Robin asked as I went in. "Can it be averted?"

Father rocked on his heels and jingled the coins in

his pockets. "I do believe Octavius has tried." Octavius being our King. "Ortis is a madman. He builds his army with single-minded purpose and, it's said, has gathered men from throughout his lands."

"While we continue to carry on as if nothing is happening," Robin put in ruefully.

"I believe King Octavius has contrived to ignore the threat. I hope not to detrimental effect."

Robin lowered his voice. "You think we will come under attack?"

"We might."

"Surely now that Prince Rupert has returned he will do something about raising our defenses?"

"So we can but hope."

"Father, you met with him at that private reception, did you not? What did you think?"

I paused, hands full of glasses, and awaited my father's response. This would make rare gossip indeed for the kitchen—not that I often joined in sharing such tidbits. Usually I just listened.

Father grunted. "He's been trained in warfare, of course. But he seems young to be in charge of an army. And if it comes to that, he will have to take his father's place. Octavius is much too ill to take the field."

"Dying?" Robin asked.

Father did glance at me then, as if noticing me for the first time. "Nearly finished there, Cindra?"

Robin, heeding me not, went on. "In your role as mayor, Father, you may be one of the few who can get near the Prince and advise him. Perhaps you might set up a meeting, seek to take his measure."

"Perhaps." Father sighed. "Your mother wishes to plan a reception. If the Prince is determined to marry—

and it seems he is—she wants to make sure his eye falls on both your sisters."

Robin groaned. "Might be a fine test, that."

"Whatever do you mean?"

"It should show us whether the Prince has any sense."

Father and Robin exchanged a look I did not entirely comprehend.

"If Rupert means to marry, he'd better do so quickly and beget an heir. His very future is uncertain. But I think he will reach higher than the daughter of a mayor. Such marriages are usually political, are they not?"

"Yes," Robin agreed, "which makes me grateful I'm not a king's son."

Chapter Four

You would not think it, but the subject of romance received much discussion in the kitchen. The maids, none of them wed, thought a good deal about marrying and leaving service. And Cook had her eye on the butcher, who often came to the door ostensibly to discuss her orders. Even I—who knew nothing about courting beyond what my sisters had imparted to me—had to admit those discussions held more flattery than details about cuts of meat.

Prudence, the head maid and the eldest among us, believed she knew much about men. She it was who went out to the market with her basket on a regular basis and bought the things Cook needed. She was also who—when Cook was well-occupied elsewhere—told the rest of us about the facts of life. Mary and Phyllis, the two other maids, listened to her with giggles.

I only half believed anything she said. She had a tongue that flapped at both ends, and most of what she told us seemed far too preposterous.

I knew men and women kissed each other. I had seen my parents kiss on rare occasions. And I supposed babies must be got somehow. It could not possibly happen the way Prudence insisted.

To listen to her, though, every male at large in the market wished to get up her skirt and perform the lewd act she described. She apparently moved from stall to stall quickly, virtually fighting them off like rabid dogs. This even though Prudence could not, by any means, be considered beautiful. She had a round, chubby face that seemed always to be greasy, and a round body to match. As she put it, men liked something on which they could get a hold.

Were Prudence to choose a husband from among these salivating suitors, she said he would have to be a man of independent means with his own thriving business. Then she could get out of the hellhole that was the kitchen.

Me, I had no hope of escaping the kitchen and no hope either of romance. I did, of course, have my books, and some of them mentioned love, but only in the most gentle and discreet manner. The *love* about which I read had absolutely no relation to anything Prudence described.

I would not wish to read of it, otherwise.

But beyond the pale, there would be no marriage for me, and no children, even though in a vague sort of way I sometimes longed for both. At least so I believed before I met the stick boy.

One of my duties—and one I enjoyed the most—was tending the kitchen garden. It gave me a chance to get outside even though, the garden being walled, I could not so much as see the street. I loved the feel of the sun on my back and the scents of the herbs Cook sent me to pick, saying the other girls' fingers were too clumsy.

In that summer rife with talk of war and lovemaking, the garden thrived. I remained knelt down among the basil the first time I saw the stick boy.

Or should I say the first time he saw me?

Tradesmen were in the habit of lifting the gate and walking into the garden directly, and thence to the door of the kitchen. The stick boy—whose name I later learned to be Nathan—first appeared on a warm afternoon and, unprecedented in the past, he paused and spoke to me.

"Who might you be, then?"

Nathan had little to recommend him beyond a wide smile. Nearly as ugly as me, he'd been newly taken on by the man who supplied kindling to the local houses.

My first glimpse showed him shabby from head to scuffed shoes. Surely no older than I, he had a squat, broad body, a crop of brown hair liberally sprinkled with bark, gapped teeth, and a face like a potato.

When I stared up from the patch of basil, failing to answer, he asked, "You the cook?"

I shook my head.

He juggled the bundle of sticks on his shoulder. "I were told to bring the kindling, miss."

Miss. Very rarely did I get such a sign of respect.

"Um," I said brilliantly. I got to my feet and brushed the dirt from my knees. His bright blue eyes followed my movements with unseemly interest.

Cook, I conjectured, must have an agreement with his master.

"Come along," I whispered. "Bring the bundle inside."

"Not so quick. You work here, right?"

I did, and so I nodded.

"Well, what's your name?"

Cinder-Ugly. The appellation had followed me into the kitchen. I lowered my head and voiced it not.

He took a step closer. "Shy, are you? I'm thinking

we can be friends. You ever been kissed?"

I stared at him in wonder. No one—not even the likes of the boot blacks—would want to kiss me.

Yet his eyes, actually very nice blue eyes, inspected my distorted face frankly before dropping to my bosom. His stare made me feel very odd indeed.

"Want to…" he had begun, when cook bellowed from the kitchen doorway.

"Get in here, girl. Who's that, then?"

Nathan—I did not know his name then—grinned at me before turning to the doorway. "Kindling, Missus."

"Leave it there beside the door and be on your way."

After that, Nathan returned every couple of days. A large kitchen requires a good amount of kindling. I figured out he usually appeared around mid-afternoon, and I tried to be in the garden, though I could not have said why.

He always paused and paid me some attention—a word or two, a grin or two, and a flattering assessment of my body. I liked the way the attention felt, addictive as Cook's cherry tarts.

Before long, though, she noticed. She waited till the maids were occupied elsewhere before sitting me down for a frank talk.

"Cindra, I've seen you with that lad."

"What lad, Cook?" Though I knew. Only one lad then occupied my world.

She said brutally, "He's not for the likes of you."

Why not? Was it because I was too ugly even for a boy who gathered sticks in the forest? One whose toes were coming through his shoes?

Every instinct told me he liked me. Feeling like I'd

been slapped down, I said nothing.

Cook sighed. “Girl, you know nothing of the world. Or boys. How could you? But boys like him, they’re after only one thing. You give it to him, you could end up with a brat in your belly. And then what would your parents say? They’ll blame me, that’s what.”

I wasn’t sure I understood. I whispered, “We just talk.”

“I know, lamb.” For once, Cook did not sound angry with me. “And who could blame you? But let me tell you: it always starts with talking. Then a kiss and a cuddle. Next thing you know, your skirts are over your head.”

“Not me,” I cried. “I’m…” I didn’t want to speak the word, not even to Cook, herself no beauty.

“Doesn’t matter,” she said roundly. “Many a plain girl’s found herself caught out. Men don’t care, see, once your skirts are up over your head.”

Well, that was a revelation. I thought my appearance always mattered, as did my mother’s and sisters’. Their lives revolved around their beauty.

“Take my warning,” Cook insisted. “You’re not my daughter nor, in truth, my employee. But I’ll tell you like I’d tell my own—do not let him talk you into anything. Has he kissed you yet?”

I shook my head wildly.

“Well, you be a good girl and keep it that way.”

“Yes, Cook.”

“Might be best if you stay in the kitchen when he comes round.”

My disappointment must have showed, for she hastily went on, “Now, I know it must feel nice having a beau, even one such as him. But you'll thank me some day, you will."

I agreed, though it was just lip service. Henceforth all I seemed able to contemplate was kissing Nathan. How would it feel? How would he taste? Would it be so terribly wrong?

Soon after that, the kitchen became very busy. Following a series of arguments between Mother and Father, most of which could be overheard, Mother won her way and planned a reception for Prince Rupert. A flurry of activity broke out through the household, people coming and going endlessly. Inevitably, Cook lost track of me.

The house seemed impossibly hectic that afternoon. Not one but two seamstresses had arrived with their entourages—I myself had admitted the second batch. Mother called Cook away to discuss a menu for the event and, knowing what time it was, I stepped out into the garden.

Nathan might well have been waiting for me. He came in through the gate as soon as I reached the herb bed and approached me directly.

"Well, lass, things seem busy here today."

"There's to be a grand reception," I told him, pleased to have something interesting to say. "The Prince will be here."

"The Prince, eh?"

"Yes. Everyone's most excited." I asked curiously, "Have you ever seen the Prince? The girls say he's ever so handsome."

Nathan stared at me. "Handsome's not everything. A boy can be pretty, sure. A man needs more than handsome."

Different from women, then. All a woman needed was to be beautiful.

"Come here and I'll show you," Nathan said, and lowered his bundle to the ground.

I shook my head.

He ignored my refusal. "A man needs to know how to please a girl."

"Yes?"

"Yes. So, you never said—have you been kissed?"

My lips parted involuntarily. I'd certainly given it a lot of thought these past days. And I'd read about it: sweet, chaste things, kisses were, between the pages of books. Marks of devotion.

"Come on, I'll show you."

Nathan seized my hand and towed me to the back of the garden, where fruit trees grew in front of the wall. What came after was lewd and sloppy and had no relationship whatever to devotion.

I suppose as a first kiss it was thorough. Nathan squeezed my breast through my gown for good measure before he asked, "You like that?"

I didn't. But having no wish to be rude, I nodded.

He bent forward to whisper in my ear, "It gets better."

His breath smelled like his mouth had tasted. For an instant I wanted to gag. I froze where I stood, like a hare in the shadow of an owl.

His eyes gleamed. "Maybe next time you'll let me touch you—up under your skirt."

My instincts shouted *no*. By then I just wanted to escape him. I drew away, gave him an uncertain look, and henceforth never went out into the garden again, at least not when I thought he might arrive.

Chapter Five

The night of the reception came with astonishing speed. Preparations overtook the household from highest to lowest, which included me. We were up from four in the morning on the day. I peeled mountains of vegetables, thinking all the while how the Prince might eat what my fingers had touched. Then I was put to work stirring gelatins and sauces, filling tiny tartlets just so, and generally being run off my feet.

Mother never came to the kitchen, though Father stopped in several times to ask if Cook had all she might need.

On one of those occasions he focused on me. "All right, Cindra?"

"Yes, sir." I never called him "Father" here.

He seemed to contemplate my appearance for a moment. "I suppose you are very excited."

I felt a lot of things, including too warm in the kitchen, but I nodded obediently.

"Have you no better clothes to wear?" he asked me inexplicably.

Cook stepped up. "Master, Mistress has given us all new clothes for tonight—just in case someone should catch sight of us. But we're not going to get them all dirtied up with *cooking*."

"No," he mused. "Hard work, isn't it?"

"Yes, Master."

"I expect Cindra would like to see the reception. She will help serve tonight, Cook. See to it she's properly groomed."

"Her? Serve?" Cook and the girls gasped.

"See to it," Father repeated and walked out.

"Well, I'll be," Cook declared.

"Why her?" Prudence whined. "I'm senior girl."

"Never mind," Cook said quickly, apparently recalling just who I was, of a sudden. "She's no clumsier than the rest of you."

Henceforth I became a bundle of nerves. Cook sent me off early to tidy myself and change. Nurse, getting wind of it, emerged from the nursery and helped me do my hair. I wore a black dress with a frilly apron and a matching bonnet, and felt quite grand.

Maybe I would see the Prince. Perhaps I would see him eat something I had touched. I could imagine nothing higher.

"Now, do not drop anything," Nurse told me in parting. A curse, no doubt.

I do not know what Father thought when he gave me the nod to serve. A treat, he likely supposed it, not more hard work. Perhaps he thought that, just as when I'd been small, I'd enjoy a glimpse of all the people, the flowers, the splendor. Maybe he overlooked how the last occasion had ended.

Truth to tell, I would have been happier keeping to my familiar domain in the kitchen. Other staff had been hired to serve. And Prudence spoke correctly—I knew nothing of the duty.

Yet the others stared at me enviously as Cook loaded me with a heavy tray and sent me forth for the first time.

A very heavy tray. The salver, made of silver and nearly two feet wide, had weight all its own. Mine, piled with the tiny tarts I'd helped prepare, made a significant load. Pushed into the reception room, I threaded my way through a myriad of guests—no easy task, given the way they were packed in—eyes down so I saw little but hems and feet.

Initially, I caught no glimpse of the Prince. I was far away from the front windows, where he received guests, and he remained a distant star. I didn't catch sight of my parents either, though I did see Nelissa preening herself and flirting with an extremely handsome young man who wore a suit of puce-colored silk.

Jostled on every side, feet stepped on, I worked my way deeper into the room. Nelissa, who wore a gorgeous gown of sky blue, shot me a startled look, touched her companion on the arm, and hurried away without acknowledging me.

Of course she would not acknowledge me—I looked and behaved like no more than a servant. Where had she gone? To tell Mother? I wondered if I should slip away now before something terrible happened. But the route behind me had closed.

And now Nelissa's former companion bent over my tray, making a selection. My arms trembled as I fought to keep the heavy tray steady, and he glanced into my face. By all the saints, he was handsome, with dark hair and the bluest eyes I'd ever seen.

Sudden envy of Nelissa flooded through me. In truth, I envied my sisters seldom, despite all they had. I'd been raised to accept that they—and I—deserved what we received. But now I experienced a sharp pang.

Why did Nelissa, with her ill temper and mean spirit, deserve a beau such as this, while the best for which I might hope was the likes of Nathan?

Nelissa's beau smiled at me. "Thank you. Move along, lass."

I obeyed, moving deeper and deeper into the room. Music played somewhere, half lost in laughter and conversation. Bodies became more densely packed, and everyone here faced one direction. I did not doubt the Prince stood somewhere ahead, and my heart began to pound.

I passed other servers, also struggling. I resolved that when all my tarts had been claimed—nearly half were now gone—I would go hide in my room.

Where I belonged.

A weed does not belong in a beautiful garden, and I should not be here. I'd defy Father's instructions and pluck myself if I had to.

It must have taken half an hour for me to push through the rest of the crowd. Suddenly it opened up before me and I saw them.

Saw him.

He stood at the front of the room, a thousand candles behind him and with my family at his side. His father, the King, must have been too ill to come, but he stood with an elegant older woman I imagined must be the Queen. My mother, wearing a grand gown crusted in gold that shone like the sun, stood on his left, Father with her. Both my sisters, along with Robin and his fiancée, were with them, all in a line.

Nelissa saw me immediately and leaned over past Father, toward Mother. With all my heart, I dreaded Mother seeing me. I tried to press back into the crowd, but I'd reached the open area just in front of the exalted guests and had no exit for the press of bodies behind.

I did not know what to do. Used to solitude or the familiar bustle of the kitchen, I felt overwhelmed. I froze, tray still in my hands.

I suppose no one could blame the Prince for thinking I offered the delicacies to him. Indeed, he stepped forward and, just as I'd dreamed earlier, selected a tartlet filled by my own hands. I raised my eyes to his face and—

How can I explain the way my first glimpse of him affected me? I have no words, not even after all my reading. He looked nothing like I'd imagined. Not handsome as was Nelissa's beau, no. Had I seen him on the street and out of the grand, sapphire blue suit he wore, I might have taken him for a horse trainer or even a broker. Some kind of businessman.

He had a long face, narrow and very tan—all that traveling, no doubt. His nose might have been too long, and his cheeks held lines that bracketed his mouth. His hair, in contrast to the tan, looked very fair, light brown streaked blond by the sun.

His eyes met mine for one long, breathless moment. *Green.*

They were green.

I'd never before seen anyone with green eyes.

"Thank you," he told me just as Nelissa's lips reached Mother's ear.

Mother looked at me and screeched like a fire siren going off at midnight. I think she cried my father's name but cannot be sure.

I dropped the tray. It fell hard with a clatter that echoed through the room. The remaining tarts—still a generous load—flew everywhere, spewing their jam fillings as they went—on the carpet, on my shoes, on the Queen's skirt, and all over the Prince's sapphire blue legs.

Everything froze. The music paused; everyone stopped talking. Into the resultant silence someone laughed in horror and said, "Oh, my God!"

Mother's face seized in a rictus; she leered at me. For an instant I could see nothing else. Not my father, not Bethessa—who, I'm pretty sure, had laughed—not even the mess that surrounded me like the fallout from an explosion.

Just her anger. Her horror. Her disgust.

Then the moment's paralysis broke. Mother reached out quick as a wasp and slapped me. The blow took me on the cheek, and its force turned my head. Instant tears flooded my eyes.

"Stupid girl!" She drew back her hand to strike again. Two things happened before she could: Father cried, "Erikka—it was my fault!" And the Prince stepped between me and my mother and seized her wrist.

"Please, Madame, do not. It was but an accident."

No rebuke colored his tone. He sounded exceedingly polite. But I knew my mother took it as a rebuke, and a public one. Her face stained with ugly red, and she transferred her glare from me to the Prince.

Even at that moment, that terrible, terrible moment, I knew she would never forgive me for this.

Eyes downcast and now kneeling on the carpet, I tried desperately to make it right. I gathered up what I could, but the tarts crumbled in my fingers, and the fillings merely spread—on the Queen's hem, her delicate slippers. All over the Prince's boots. My efforts only made things worse.

But the music resumed playing, and people started up talking and laughing. The world had, apparently, not ended.

Engaged in my efforts, I missed much of what went on over my head. I thought Mother and the Prince engaged in a low conversation. Father touched my shoulder, but I couldn't stand, wouldn't stand. Adrift in a sea of humiliation, I wanted only to fall through the carpet.

Then someone crouched down beside me. At first I thought he was Robin. But I caught a glimpse of sapphire blue knee beside my own and looked up directly into green eyes.

"It's all right," he said. "I do things like this all the time. Please don't cry."

I stared in astonishment and choked out, "Your suit—"

His lips curved in a wry smile; the lines in his cheeks deepened. "It needed a bit more decoration, don't you think? Not garish enough on its own."

I moved at lightning speed from horror to delight. I adored dry wit, even if most of my exposure so far had been on the written page.

For one priceless moment, we smiled at one another.

Then fingers seized my ear. I was hauled up from my knees to face my mother.

"Go to your room," she seethed. "Await your punishment."

The Prince surged to his feet also. "Madame, it is a trifle, an accident. She meant no harm."

I don't think Mother even heard him. She would have struck me then and there had Father not stepped forward and intervened. "Erikka, you're making a scene."

Nothing could be better calculated to bring her to her senses. She drew herself together, and I fled, abandoning my tray and the mess, threading my way through the crowded chamber and thence up the stairs at a stumbling run to my chamber.

Where I waited.

Chapter Six

My mother never came till the next morning. To be fair, the reception didn't end till daylight, and I'm sure she had many other things to which she needed to attend.

No one else came near me, not even Nurse. The waiting proved hard, but I had hope that with the passage of time Mother's rage might abate.

It did not.

She came armed with a leather strap and ordered me off the bed to my feet. She berated me at top volume, accompanying every insult with a blow. I turned my back in an effort to protect my face, and was on my knees before Father—followed by Robin—broke into the room.

"For God's sake, Erikka! Have you lost your mind?" He seized hold of her and wrested away the strap, which he passed to Robin. "Do you want to kill her?"

Mother began to weep. "I *will* kill her if she's spoiled her sisters' chances with the Prince. One of my daughters is to be a princess, do you hear?"

Father shook her. "Listen to me! No one knows she's their sister. And it was all my fault. I sent her in to serve."

Swift as a striking terror, she slapped him. "Fool! You knew I had ambitions."

Robin hissed. He came and helped me up from the floor and inspected my stripes. “She will need a physician,” he said.

“No!” Mother wailed. “No one can see…”

Robin’s and Father’s eyes met.

“Come, Erikka,” Father said then. “You need a powder to calm you. Robin, fetch Nurse to tend your sister’s injuries.”

I lay face down on my bed and wept till Nurse came. Robin did not stay to see what came next; Nurse and I were alone. She—neither kind nor harsh—clucked her tongue all the while she tended my hurts, pronouncing it as her opinion that I would have scars, and left me alone with my misery.

That my mental ache superseded the physical, I could not deny. I had failed. It seemed I did so perpetually. Father had trusted me with a simple task, and I had disappointed him, enraged Mother, and showered both the Queen and the Prince with pastry.

The Prince.

I could scarcely bear to think of him. Those green eyes. The way he had come to my aid. His kindness. I wept throughout the morning for a multitude of reasons.

And then in the afternoon there came a ruckus from downstairs, only faintly heard at the top of the house. My mother’s voice sounded again. Father’s as well. Once more, they argued.

Soon Father returned to my room. My stripes had stiffened by then, and it hurt to breathe, let alone swivel around on the bed to face him. But astonishment took away some of the sting.

He wore a tentative look and bore a small nosegay in his hand.

"Cindra, these have arrived. For you."

"What?" I could not comprehend. Flowers arrived in profusion for both my sisters, never for me.

"From Prince Rupert." Father looked nearly as surprised as I felt. But he passed the bouquet into my hands.

Violets there were, and tiny pink rosebuds, and the most delicate calendulas, and…well, something fragrant, like thyme. The scent surrounded me.

"There's a note. He sent a note," Father stammered. "I've read it. He hopes you are no worse for your mishap last night—" Here Father faltered; I was very much worse.

"Cindra, I'm sorry. It was my fault. I should have realized you're not trained to serve. I merely wished for you to share in some of the excitement."

I barely heard Father's words. The Prince had sent me flowers, this delicate and most perfect little bouquet. Even though he thought me a servant.

I unfolded the note, which had been tied to the bouquet with purple ribbon. Purple, my favorite color.

I hope you are fully recovered from our shared mishap last evening and will not give it another thought. Best regards, Rupert Octavius.

Rupert Octavius. He had signed his name in a clear, black hand. Or perhaps whoever had made up the bouquet—I certainly didn't possess sufficient naiveté to think he'd done it himself—had written it. Yet he'd thought of me. Gone out of his way to send these. A kind gesture.

"You know," Father said, "none of us could be sure what to expect from Prince Rupert. He has been away so long, a mere boy when he went off to begin his education. And with his father so ill, and facing this threat of war, he will prove pivotal to our future. But I'm impressed. He's…"

Father paused, apparently at a loss for words.

"Kind," I supplied.

"Yes. And there's strength in him. Not flashy strength, but it's there, like a backbone of steel."

I nodded. The door of my room opened, and Robin slipped in. He asked Father, "Have you told her?"

"I thought I'd leave it to you, son."

I stared at them in bewilderment as Robin came forward and sat on the edge of my bed. Father moved to close the door.

"What is it?" I asked.

Robin gazed at me a moment before he replied; I thought I saw sorrow in his dark eyes. "Cindra, you know I'm to wed in a month."

"Yes."

"Once Donella and I are married, we will have our own household. I would like you to come and live with us there."

"As a servant, you mean?"

Unaccountably, Robin's eyes filled with tears. "No, as my sister and a member of our family."

I gaped, not knowing what to say.

"I will need to discuss it with Donella, of course," Robin went on, "but I cannot imagine her objecting. One of the things I value most in her is her compassionate heart."

I glanced at Father. "But—but I live here. I work in the kitchen. You—you need me."

Father looked away.

"Donella and I will need you, too," Robin told me.

"I hope—pray—children will come along soon. And if the future goes badly and I am forced to enlist, I would be happier knowing I do not leave Donella alone."

Completely at a loss, I laid the bouquet on my knee and raised my hands. "I do not know how…"

"You'll learn," Robin assured me.

Father moved closer. "Look, Cindra, you can stay here no longer. Your mother's treatment of you has demonstrated that. You will have a better, more appropriate life with Robin."

Appropriate? What was appropriate for me? I had no way to measure, no way to imagine.

I opened my mouth; no words came, so I shut it again.

Robin stood up from the edge of the bed. "Allow me to speak with Donella. Meanwhile, you concentrate on healing."

"Mother—"

Father said, "You will not be seeing your mother again. I have forbidden her from coming here. Or to the kitchen."

He had forbidden. But no one forbade Mother anything. Neither her nor my sisters.

"But," I said, "even if I live with Robin"—an unimaginable prospect; a different household. A different bedroom. I'd never known anything but the nursery and this. "It's a month away. Surely I will see Mother before then."

"Leave that to me," Father said. "As Robin suggests, you concentrate on healing."

"My flowers," I whispered. "They will need water."

"Surely you have water here?"

I shook my head.

Father frowned. "I will send one of the maids directly with a vase."

"And I," said Robin with fake cheer, "am off to see my fiancée."

I cannot begin to describe my feelings once they'd gone. Amazed, uncertain—a bit grateful, but wholly fearful. Mother's strap seemed to have rent not only my skin but my world.

It was dark before Robin returned. By then I'd been brought a vase full of water by a scowling Prudence and even a tray containing a bowl of sops in milk, one of the few times my supper had ever been served to me.

I was reading, with my bouquet on the table beside me, when Robin knocked and came in. All afternoon I'd been busy assuring myself Donella would refuse to have me in her household. Why should she want a freak like me under her roof, someone used to spending her time in the cinders of the kitchen fire?

Cinder-Ugly. I heard the taunt in my sisters' voices again. Surely I would be left here at their mercy, all I'd ever been able to imagine for myself.

Robin sat down and looked at me gravely. I felt doubly sure then that his fiancée had refused. But he said with sorrow, "I am ashamed to say Donella did not realize I have a third sister."

"Oh."

"We spent these past hours discussing the situation here and how you have lived your life. The long and short of it is she will be pleased to welcome you into our home."

Heat and cold rushed over me in turns. It seemed

there should be something I must say—"thank you," perhaps. But I didn't feel grateful.

"But, but," I stammered, "I don't know how to *be*."

"I understand that, as does Donella. I want the two of you to meet. She will help you order a wardrobe."

"A what?"

"Some proper clothes. Visitors who come into our home will meet you as a member of our family. Not a maid."

I twisted my fingers together. "I can't do this."

"You can, Cindra. One step at a time."

****

I met Donella two days later, in the tiny sitting room at the back of my father's house. Difficult to imagine I'd only seen her from a distance before, once at the reception when I'd dropped the tray. Now she entered the room on a wave of lavender scent, a stunning vision.

Donella had jet black hair and deep blue eyes, cheeks like roses, and a dimpled smile. She wore an ivory-colored gown and a pelisse of blue that matched her eyes. But the loveliest thing about her, so I thought, was the kind manner in which she looked at me.

Robin escorted her in, and she sat in a chair facing me. I wondered what she thought—if, facing me in the flesh, she would change her mind about giving me house room.

But after shooting a look at Robin, she smiled. "Hello, Cindra. I'm so pleased to meet you. I understand you've had a very bad time."

I wondered to what she referred. The recent beating? The humiliation of tossing a tray of tarts all over the Prince and the Queen? My life in general?

"I hope," Donella went on when I did not reply, "you'll be comfortable living with us. And I hope you and I will be friends."

Friends?

Somehow I found my voice. "Are you sure?"

"What, dear?"

"Are you sure you want to take me in?"

Robin answered. "Cindra, I am ashamed of what has taken place in this house. Please allow me and Donella to make it up to you. Sister, your life is about to get better."

He was wrong—all our lives were about to fall apart.

Chapter Seven

The time until my brother's wedding passed in a blur of activity. Much still needed to be done, and I became part of it.

Donella came to Father's home often and always met with me in the back parlor. There she helped me decide what clothing I needed to order for my new life and helped me through the humiliation of being seen by the seamstress—something I'd never before endured. I barely spoke during these meetings. To communicate with the seamstress, who brought drawings and samples, I would whisper words to Donella, who then passed my choices along.

A conversation might go something like this…

Donella: Which of these fabric swatches do you like, Cindra?

Me: The purple.

Donella: Yes? And the lavender lace?

Me: It's beautiful. But not for me.

Donella to the seamstress: We'll have one made up in both these colors. Oh, and the teal. I think that will look very well.

I became used to Donella with her steady, cheerful kindness, but facing anyone else still felt impossible.

On the day she came and asked me to be a bridesmaid, I lost what little composure I'd attained.

"I would love for you to be part of our wedding,"

she told me by way of persuasion. "And I think there's still time for your gown to be prepared, if we decide at once."

I broke down in tears even though I rarely wept in front of anyone, having learned long ago it did me no good. "I can't!" I wailed.

"Oh, my dear, I didn't mean to make you cry. Robin and I merely wanted you to feel part of things. But I can quite see it would be difficult."

I raised a face made still uglier by tears. "You must want your wedding to be beautiful."

"Yes, of course."

"I want it to be beautiful. My sisters will be standing up for you, yes?"

"Yes."

"I cannot, simply cannot, stand up beside them. They are beautiful. I am ugly."

"Cindra—"

"And Mother will be there! If she sees I am part of the wedding, she will become enraged, scream, and make a scene."

Iron entered Donella's sweet voice. "You suppose I am unwilling to face up to her on your behalf?"

"I could not bear it." And that was the truth. The very prospect made me want to crawl away and hide.

"Very well. I understand. Dry your tears. You don't need to do anything that frightens you so. But say you will be there! In the back of the church, perhaps?"

"If she sees me there—"

Donella bit her lip. "Yes, all right. Forgive me, Cindra. I didn't mean to upset you."

I wailed, "No, forgive me! You've been so kind. I do not wish to disappoint you."

"There's no disappointment on my part. I am marrying the man of my dreams, and everything else is frosting on the cake. I do not suppose you can face the reception either?"

I shook my head violently.

Donella touched the back of my hand, which had been caught by Mother's strap. "As you wish, dear. We'll ease into things, shall we?"

I squeezed my eyes shut and nodded, not sure I could face the future after all.

****

By all accounts, the wedding proved a grand spectacle and a great success. I watched from the top of the stairs as everyone left—my sisters both clad in soft green and Mother in deep rose—and saw them return again following the reception. In between, the house seemed unusually quiet, with everyone, including the kitchen staff, gone off to attend. Only the aged butler and I remained.

I had never before been alone in the house. No one to hear me—for old Karl was mostly deaf—and no one to see me, either. I wandered from room to room, peering out windows and fantasizing this was my own home.

Up in my room, my few belongings had been packed up, for I would move to Robin's house the day after tomorrow and await the return of the newlyweds from their honeymoon. Most of my new wardrobe would be delivered to Robin's house also, though I did wear one gown, finished in tiny sprigs of green with purple flowers. It reminded me of my bouquet, now long dead and pressed between the pages of my favorite book. That would also travel with me.

I spent a while standing in front of the mirror in the drawing room, where the light fell mercilessly, gazing at myself in my new gown. To me, I looked like a scrawny chicken clad in a dress of borrowed feathers. Still just a chicken in disguise. Still ugly.

Donella had tried to show me how to arrange my hair, but to little effect. My hair, too limp and lifeless to do anything but lie on my neck, refused to hold a curl.

I wondered if I did the right thing, venturing out into the world. I wondered what my mother thought of the development. She had not been near me since the day of the beating; Father must have kept her away.

But surely she understood that at Robin's house I would pass beyond her control. She wouldn't be able to keep people outside the family from seeing me. Robin and Donella might well have visitors. They'd given no indication they meant to do anything other than introduce me as Robin's sister.

Word would get out that Erikka Bulgar had an ugly daughter. That possibility must terrify Mother as much as it did me.

How had Father brought her to accept it?

I received an answer to that question later, when everyone returned from the wedding reception.

The house had been so quiet all those hours it seemed like a sudden storm breaking when they came in. I heard my sisters' voices first, chattering like birds, and Father's rumble. But it was Mother's voice, hollering my name wildly, that sent a chill down my spine.

She called for me. She never called for me. I stood at the top of the stairs, peering down, saw them gathered like a bright bouquet in the foyer, and wondered whether to run. But she looked up and saw me, and waved an imperious hand.

“There she is. Get down here.”

“Erikka,” Father began, and seized her elbow.

She shrugged him off. “Leave me alone. I will have my say before she leaves this house.”

I started down slowly. I will admit I didn’t realize at once that Mother had taken too much to drink. Perhaps I should have; a wedding, after all, is a celebration, and the drink probably flowed freely. I had often seen Mother with a goblet in her hands while entertaining, but never drunk so it showed.

Now she watched me descend the stairs, her head thrown back. By the time I reached her, a sneer contorted her face.

“Look at you,” she seethed. “All dressed up. Doesn’t help much, does it? You’re still ugly.”

“Erikka,” Father said again.

I did not speak, did not attempt to answer her. I knew I still looked hideous; I’d spent the afternoon assuring myself of it. And, on some level, I sensed she’d decided to destroy me here and now, before I passed beyond her reach. Perhaps she thought if she reduced me far enough I would never again raise my head, never show myself at Robin’s house and embarrass her.

Nelissa and Bethessa giggled. One glance into their faces told me they intended to enjoy this scene.

“Cinder-Ugly,” one of them whispered—Bethessa, I thought. “Fit only to live among the cinders.”

“Yes, but”—Mother took it up swiftly—“she has grand ideas about herself. Your brother has encouraged that, curse him.”

"Mother…" I began desperately.

Her face twisted into a mask of cruelty. As always when she directed her bile at me, she became ugly too—this most lovely of women. I wondered suddenly if that was why she hated me so much, because my ugliness made hers evident.

"Do not call me that! Do not ever call me that. You are no daughter of mine, do you understand? I have two daughters, and they are both lovely. Here you see them! You were an error, an ab-ab-aberration. I should have strangled you at birth."

"Erikka!" Father cried for the third time. He caught her shoulders between his hands and spoke into her face. "How can you say such a dreadful thing?"

"It's the truth. I have given her house room all this while. Now she thinks she will go out into the world and ruin me!"

"I won't," I whispered.

"What?" Mother's head spun back toward me.

"It speaks!" Nelissa said.

"I won't tell anyone I'm your daughter," I shouted. "I won't!" I'd never before raised my voice at my mother. At my sisters, yes, when younger and they taunted me. But the pain inside me now demanded release.

She narrowed her eyes and hissed, "Stupid, stupid girl. It will get out. How do you think it won't?"

"I'll hide. In my room. Just like always."

Mother broke free from Father's grasp and stepped toward me. She swayed as she came, and only then did I see her intoxication. She came up close, closer than she'd been in years, so I could smell the drink on her breath.

For one suspended moment I thought she might soften after all, accept my offer of self-abasement, and relent.

Instead, she whispered words for my ear alone. “There’s only one thing you can do to please me, girl—go away and take your own life.”

Chapter Eight

I never told anyone what Mother said to me there at the foot of the stairs. Nobody else heard, and Mother fell down immediately after, too drunk to stand. Father helped her away, and my sisters went off snickering.

I returned to my room, feeling like I'd been stabbed to the heart. I didn't try to rationalize what had taken place or blame Mother's words on the drink she'd consumed. There is truth in wine, as the books say. She had at last expressed her fondest wish for me.

If she wanted to reduce me beyond the pale, she succeeded. By the time I departed for Robin's house, I could scarcely lift my gaze from the floor. It didn't help that Robin and Donella remained away a week longer. I relocated to the new room they'd prepared for me and hid there as I always had, making of it simply a far more beautiful prison.

Donella had done up the room in soft lavender, with white curtains and bed hangings. She'd given me glossy white bookcases for my treasured volumes, a soft patterned carpet, and a chair for reading. The windows overlooked the back garden, or more precisely what Donella hoped would be the back garden once she had time to work on it. Walled with warm orange brick, that space beckoned to me, but I dared not go down.

I did not want anyone to see me. I took my meals in my room and encountered only two servants.

Did I think about the request Mother made of me? I thought about very little else. The one thing I could do for her, it would ease her pain and shame over my existence. I didn't doubt she felt shame for having produced such a monster.

But I didn't know how I might accomplish the deed. I could slit my wrists, but I didn't have a knife. I might throw myself from the window to the stones below, but I feared the fall might not kill me. I might be left even more broken and a burden to those I loved.

I decided the most likely prospect lay in hanging. My bedding could be twisted into a rope. If I secured it somehow to the top of the window frame, I could drop out the window and end my life. It would not be an easy death, but I had no reason to believe I deserved easy.

I deserved nothing.

The thing that stopped me, other than sheer cowardice, was a lack of means to secure the makeshift noose. Again, if I merely fell, I might become a worse burden than I was now.

"Miss, would you like me to do your hair?"

Little Gerta, who'd been assigned to me as maid, often interrupted my dire thoughts. Barely older than I, and a tiny thing, she could not be called beautiful either, having a plain, freckled face and that undersized frame. But her brown eyes remained kind and she never, by word or deed, showed any sign of judging me.

She hauled water for my bath, brushed my clothing, and attempted to dress my hair, all while speaking gently. She brought me trays of food and took them away again barely touched. She never questioned my refusal to leave the room.

I wondered if Donella had warned her about me. It was difficult to tell.

She brushed my hair at length—one hundred strokes, as she said—and twisted it up on top of my head, held with jeweled pins, calling it "becoming." When she helped me with my bath—a hot bath had become my single pleasure—she never commented on the welts on my back. For Mother's beating had indeed left scars—not from every bite of the strap, only the deepest.

Gerta might ask me softly about the latest book I'd read or ask if I'd like flowers brought up to my room. If she brought flowers, she always included some purple blooms. She never looked at me as if I didn't deserve to live.

Then Donella and Robin returned, and life changed once again. They both came to my room to greet me, fresh from their journey. They looked wonderful, Donella's cheeks abloom and Robin wearing a new gravity that suited him. Donella embraced me and asked how I liked my chamber.

I assured her I did, and she expressed herself as glad.

"But," she said, "I do not want you to feel confined here. That was never our intention when we invited you to live with us, was it, Robin?"

"No, indeed," my brother said.

Gently, Donella pressed, "I hope you will come downstairs and dine with us."

"I can't." I dropped my eyes. Someone might see me. He or she might put word about, and that would get back to Mother.

"Nonsense. It will be just the three of us this

evening, right, Robin? You need not see any guests till you feel ready."

"I…" I could think of no excuse.

Donella brightened. "You must hear all about our wedding trip. Oh, how many times I wished you were there with us to see the sights. Wait till I tell you about the Uphill Road and the Tomb of Queen Esmerelda."

I wanted to hear. I looked shyly at my brother, who smiled at me. "You'd better let her share it all, Cindra, or she'll burst."

Donella went on, "Put on one of your new dresses. Surely they've all arrived by now."

They had. I'd unpacked them and hung them all in the big wardrobe.

Robin put in, "Cindra, this will be a private supper just for the three of us. A good place for you to begin."

How could I explain how uncomfortable the prospect made me feel? How remind him I'd only once shared in a family supper? They tried so hard to be kind.

I nodded. They went away, and Gerta appeared at my side.

"Miss, which gown would you like to wear?"

I waved a hand. "Any. Any of them."

She selected a dress in pale yellow, the color of tender primroses. She dressed me as one might a mannequin and from somewhere magically produced a genuine primrose to pin in my hair.

"There, now. How fine you look!"

Reluctantly, I raised my eyes to the glass. The girl there looked like a plucked chicken with a primrose on its head.

I went down to supper and listened to tales of

grand castles, stunning gardens, and exotic locales, Donella and Robin talking over each other in their eagerness to share all. They laughed and teased one another, and I relaxed enough to eat a few bites and smile over the story of a monkey that had climbed onto Robin's head.

That proved the first of many suppers we took together. They always included me when they were alone and invited me when they had guests, which proved often. As a young, lively couple, they loved to entertain, but with an eye to Mother's well-being, I excluded myself from such gatherings.

Robin also held a number of more serious meetings. Now well stuck into business, he often welcomed other businessmen—and men of influence—to discuss the health of the realm, its King, and the likelihood of war.

I never knew he'd become close with Prince Rupert until I bumped into the Prince unexpectedly one afternoon. I suppose it made sense; they were nearly of an age, and Rupert needed advisors he could trust. I spent so much time in my room and in the garden, where Donella had requested my help, I never paused to question the identity of my brother's guests.

On this afternoon, though, it rained, and I ran downstairs to fetch the book I'd been reading, left behind in the sitting room. I quite literally careened into someone who stood just inside the door of the chamber—his hands came out and steadied me.

Recoiling violently, I looked up and encountered a pair of green eyes that, to my horror, I identified immediately.

I froze. The eyes narrowed quizzically, and he said

with faultless politeness, "I do beg your pardon," even though it had been entirely my fault.

Dull heat raced over me, a blush that came from my deepest depths. Before I could speak, he recognized me. His face transformed in a smile.

"Why, it is the wee lass from Master Bulgar's reception. I never did learn your name."

I do not think I could have replied to save my life. His hands still rested lightly on my shoulders, and he stood so near I could catch his scent. He smelled of sunshine, despite the rain.

"Do you work here now?" he asked kindly.

Robin appeared from nowhere. Quite possibly he'd been in the room all the time and I had failed to notice him. He said, "Your Highness, this is my sister."

The Prince's eyebrows flew up. "Your sister?" he repeated. I could almost see the thoughts moving in his mind. He'd encountered a servant at my parents' house. It did not make sense to him.

"Prince Rupert," Robin said formally, "may I present the youngest of my sisters, Mistress Cindra Bulgar."

"Mistress Bulgar, charmed." Rupert slid his fingers down my arm, captured my hand, and kissed the back of it, giving a bow. I do not know how I kept from falling down on the spot.

"Thank you for the flowers," I whispered.

"I beg your pardon?" He tipped his ear toward me.

"The flowers you sent—I never received any before, and they were lovely. I treasured them."

His smile once more transfigured his face, turning it from still and grave to full of beautiful light. "I'm glad I was able to please you."

He still had hold of my hand; I struggled to keep from swooning.

He declared, "You should have flowers every day, since you enjoy them so much."

"Sending them was…kind of you." Beyond kind, but I didn't say that.

Robin said, "Cindra, why don't you stay and have tea with us? We were just going to discuss a few matters, nothing that should bore you too much."

"I can't, really. I just came to get my book." I drew my hand from Rupert's and snatched the little tome from a side table.

"Mistress Bulgar, do you like to read?"

"Yes, Your Highness."

"As do I. Many a good book kept me company on my travels about the world. We will have to compare our favorites some time."

I dropped a half curtsy and bent my head. Little did I know, when Nurse drilled us endlessly in that exercise, I would ever practice it before royalty.

Then I fled. I heard Rupert say something to Robin as I went, but I couldn't hear what.

And I felt glad I couldn't.

Chapter Nine

A spell of beautiful weather ensued. Donella and I spent all our time in the garden, dressed in our oldest clothing. First we cleared away the overgrowth, with the assistance of an aging gardener borrowed from Donella's parents. Then we sat for hours going over plans and drawings, designing how the enclosed space should look. Donella seemed to value my opinion and to enjoy my company.

I loved the enclosed yard—drowsy with warmth and the droning of bees, it felt safe to me, maybe the first truly safe space I'd ever inhabited. My family seemed impossibly distant; my mother almost ceased to exist.

I sometimes forgot my appearance. When Donella and I laughed together over some silliness, I could overlook the fact that I looked any less perfect than she.

We were engaged in just such silliness when next the Prince came to visit. We'd been busy pulling weeds out by the roots, falling over ourselves and each other, ending up liberally sprinkled with soil. Donella's eyes looked merry and, wholly engaged, I failed to immediately notice the man who walked toward us down the path.

Until he spoke: "Is this not an enchanting scene for a lovely afternoon?"

I choked on a giggle and turned, not believing the

evidence of my eyes.

But Donella laughed. "Why, thank you, Your Highness. You catch us in the middle of our grand project. It does not look much right now, but I promise you it will be magnificent in the end."

"It looks to prove a veritable oasis of beauty. And please call me Rupert, both of you."

He fixed his green eyes on me and bowed. "I confess, Mistress Bulgar, I hoped to find you today." He smiled crookedly and from behind his back swept a bouquet. "For you."

Much larger than the first bouquet he'd sent, this one had tall yellow flowers like stars and pink ones that cascaded down over his hand, and tiny blue ones like pieces of the sky.

"Oh!" I gasped and pressed my hands to my cheeks. "How lovely!"

Donella laughed kindly. "So they are. You might wish to accept them."

I reached for the bunch of flowers. My fingers brushed those of the Prince as he handed them to me.

"How very thoughtful," Donella said.

Rupert smiled. "Soon you will be surrounded by flowers and won't need my offerings. But I thought Mistress Bulgar should have an abundance of what she enjoys."

"We were just about to take a rest and share some lemonade here in the garden," Donella said. "Will you join us?"

"I would be most pleased. I am waiting for your husband, who has another appointment, and frankly I can't think of a more delightful way to spend the time."

"I will go tell the maid to bring some refreshments.

Cindra, please entertain the Prince while I am gone."

She swept off—*How could she?*—effectively dropping me into confusion.

"So, Mistress Bulgar," Prince Rupert said, "do you enjoy gardening as much as reading?"

"I do."

"Let us sit here in the sunshine. Such a peaceful place."

"It is."

I perched on the edge of the dilapidated bench—one of the things Donella planned to replace—and he seated himself at the other end. His lively green eyes inspected me before, perhaps noticing my extreme discomfort, he gazed away across the expanse.

"On my tour, I was privileged to see some of the most beautiful gardens in the world. Gardens are prized as sacred spaces in many cultures. Sitting here in the sunlight, one can see why."

I let the breath escape my lungs. "That must have been wonderful."

"I wish I might show you. If I ever go again, I promise to bring you a plant from some far place. I don't doubt even the most exotic would thrive in this sheltered spot, under your care."

"I would like that." I looked at the bouquet in my hands and not at him, marveling that I seemed to be having a conversation with a man. A prince.

"Of course I don't contemplate traveling any time soon, given my father's ill health and our perilous situation."

"Is the King very ill?"

"I fear he's dying."

Startled, I lifted my eyes to his and beheld his

sorrow.

"I'm so sorry."

"You know, Mistress Bulgar, I spent so many years away, being educated and seeing the world—both things upon which he insisted—I feel I barely know him. It will be hard on my mother. They've had a good marriage, the kind I would like for myself."

My cheeks flamed. Before I could think of an answer, Donella returned leading a maid who carried a tray containing not only the promised lemonade but dainty cakes.

The two of them chatted casually until Robin appeared to collect the Prince, when Donella said, "Your Highness, I hope you will consider this place your sanctuary and visit often."

"I would like that, Madame."

"You can follow our progress as Cindra and I transform it."

He bowed and followed Robin away. Donella looked at me thoughtfully.

"Well, that was pleasant, wasn't it, dear?"

I nodded.

"You did splendidly. Of course, I do not find Prince Rupert particularly intimidating. Do you?"

A shake of my head.

"Good. Perhaps you will not be too uncomfortable joining us when we have him to dinner. He and Robin are becoming fast friends. I anticipate His Highness will be here often."

"Oh, I couldn't…"

"Why?"

"My appearance—"

"You have all those lovely gowns. Besides, look at

you now—look at both of us. Wearing our oldest dresses and covered with soil. But he seemed to enjoy his visit, didn't he?"

"I…must go put my flowers in water."

"Do that," Donella agreed. "We would not want anything to happen to such fragile blooms."

****

After that, a bouquet arrived for me every day, sometimes small and delicate, sometimes large and exuberant. None ever had a note attached stating who sent them, but I knew.

I knew.

The most beautiful blooms I'd ever seen, they filled my bedroom and spilled over to other chambers.

Then one day the Prince arrived in person. He came wearing a dark suit with golden braid and bearing a cluster of golden flowers more exotic than any I'd ever imagined.

Donella and I, both attending to our sewing in the parlor, since it rained outside, rose to our feet. Rupert approached me directly and placed the flowers in my hands.

"Mistress Bulgar, I wished to bring these to you so that I might explain what they are. These grow in the garden of the Sun Emperor, and only there. I first saw them when I visited his citadel during my travels. Only take a breath of their perfume, if you will."

I bent over the bouquet obediently; a warm, heady essence rose to meet me, the very scent of sunshine.

"Oh!" I could not help but smile.

"How marvelous," said Donella. "Your Highness, however did you come by them?"

"I needed to send a messenger to that part of the

world and asked him to try and bring me back a few blooms. I must say, Mistress Bulgar, your smile makes it more than worth the trouble."

Emotions such as I'd never before experienced swamped me. Warmth, comfort, gratification. For the first time in my life, I felt truly valued.

"Your Highness, will you stay and take some refreshment?" Donella asked.

"I'm afraid I cannot. I'm on my way to a state reception and just stopped in to deliver those." He tipped his head. "I don't suppose, Mistress Bulgar, you would care to accompany me?"

"To a reception?"

"Yes."

"I couldn't possibly." Mother might be there. My sisters might. I sought desperately for a viable excuse. "I—I am not dressed."

"Of course. I should have afforded you more notice. Perhaps next time?"

What could I say? There he stood, magnificent from head to toe, requesting my company. Mine. Cinder-Ugly.

"I—would be honored."

"As would I." He bowed again, bid Donella good day, and left the parlor.

I sank into the nearest chair, the exotic flowers in my hands.

For several long moments neither Donella nor I spoke. Then I said brokenly, "Of course I can never go. Mother might see me. At the very least, she'd find out."

"That's not fair." Donella stamped her foot. "Cindra, she no longer controls your life."

"You don't understand. She does."

"No, you're free of her now."

I shook my head. The golden flowers blurred before my eyes.

Donella came and knelt in front of me. "Cindra, dear, he likes you."

"No."

"He does. He got you those flowers and brought them to you with his own hands."

I could feel my heart breaking. "He's wonderful. But he's the Prince. Donella—look at me."

"*He's* been looking at you, dear. It hasn't turned him away."

"How could I accompany him to a reception, or anywhere? I'm clumsy. I'd drop my food. Trip. Say the wrong thing. There are scores of pitfalls."

"I think we need to order you a ball gown. Lavender, I imagine. Or no—gold. Look how the color of those flowers warms your eyes. A glorious, golden gown."

"No." I seized her hand. "I can't do it, Donella. I never can."

I think Robin spoke with the Prince after that—explained about me. He must have filled Rupert in on at least some of the details of my background, for though Rupert continued to visit the house often and sometimes stayed for dinner, he did not press his invitation to any upcoming event.

He continued to treat me gently and kindly, and while in his company I sometimes forgot about how ugly I was.

Chapter Ten

My father visited Robin's house on occasion, my mother and sisters never. Once or twice Robin and Donella went to affairs at my parents' home; I never went along. My one happiness—outside of Donella's company and seeing the Prince—lay in the garden, which reached completion before the end of that summer.

By then we'd learned that Donella was expecting. She bloomed like one of her own flowers, becoming even more beautiful, her eyes shining and her skin aglow. We spent most of each day in the garden, where she chatted while she watched me work; I no longer let her do any heavy lifting. We spoke of names for the child and decorations for the nursery, and ignored the increasing rumors of war.

Then one evening Donella and Robin returned from dinner at my parents' and came directly to me.

"Dear," said Donella, "there is something we must tell you. Your mother is unwell."

"Is it the ague?" She used to take that badly at least once a year.

"No. Something quite other than that, I'm afraid."

"Just tell her," Robin said. "Perhaps she'll appreciate the irony."

I looked at him askance. His voice carried the hard edge it always assumed, now, when he spoke of

Mother.

Donella sat down beside me. “Several weeks ago, she put herself in the hands of a surgeon and went under the knife.”

I didn’t understand. “Why?”

Robin answered tersely, “Apparently, she no longer believed her face to be perfect. She found a surgeon willing to take a stitch here and make a tuck there.”

“She had an operation? On her face?” But Mother’s face epitomized perfection—nose narrow and regal, blue eyes set slightly atilt in a complexion like pale rose petals.

“Yes, and the procedure went badly. There’s a reason none of her regular doctors would agree to touch her. Now she’s taken an infection and is quite ill.”

“She stayed in her bed the whole time we were there,” Donella added. “We did go up and see her. She is very swollen and unhappy. The point is she won’t be attending any functions for a while. You might accompany Rupert, if you will.”

“He has stopped asking me.”

“Only because I explained to him how things stand between you and Mother,” Robin told me. “Oh, not the details. But he understands there’s been a break between the two of you and you don’t wish to encounter her.”

“I still can’t…Bethessa and Nelissa…”

“Are you going to let them run your life? Don’t you think they’ve hurt you enough?”

“I couldn’t. I can’t possibly face them.”

Robin sighed. “Forgive me, but I believe Mother’s got exactly what she deserves. And both Nelissa and

Bethessa are riding for a fall. They've thrown themselves at Rupert relentlessly, and it won't be long before he puts them in their places and no mistake." Robin's dark eyes met mine. "Neither of them has what he wants. I believe he knows exactly what he wants."

"What's that?" I whispered.

"Someone with whom he can be at ease, comfortable. A woman with whom he need not be the Prince every moment of his life."

"I hope he finds her. He deserves to be happy," I said devoutly.

"Idiot," Robin said fondly. "Can't you see the truth? He's not sending any other woman in the kingdom flowers every day."

I stumbled to my feet. "Oh, no. I…"

"Don't push her, Robin," said Donella at the same moment. "She must do this in her own time."

"Yes, I know." Robin shook his head. "I still say Mother has much for which to answer."

"She's answering for it now," Donella told him, "in the most painful way."

****

All that night I thought about what they'd said and what Robin had implied, and rejected the implication whole. Rupert—Prince of all the land and soon to be King—could not possibly be interested in me. Not but I might wish him to be. But such dreams simply did not come true. Anyway, it would prove half dream and half nightmare. How could I possibly be what such a man needed?

The next day, Robin left the house to attend a business meeting, and Donella went to her mother's to plan a layette. Alone in the garden, I attempted to sort through my troubled thoughts. No sooner had I begun to relax, however, than one of the servants showed Rupert into the space.

Looking up to see him approach me down the flagged path, I couldn't prevent a smile of delighted surprise. "Oh, hello!"

He gave a slight bow and waited for the maid to move away before he said, "Mistress Bulgar, I have come crying sanctuary."

"I beg your pardon?"

"I need somewhere to hide for a time, away from the generals and the statesmen and all the others clamoring for my ear. Naturally, I thought of this place. It is the very heart of peace."

"It is, isn't it?" I couldn't help but agree. "Especially on such a morning as this." I nodded sympathetically. "Of course you are welcome, Your Highness. Stay as long as you like."

"Thank you kindly. And here, for a time, might I not cease to be 'Highness'? Do you think I might just be Rupert while we talk together?"

"Well, if you like." I began to climb to my feet, but he forestalled me.

"No, don't rise—you make far too lovely a picture there among the flowers, with the sun on your hair."

I froze. Me, a lovely picture? Surely not. While working in the garden, I always wore my oldest gowns. My hands bore a coating of dirt, and my hair, never well-behaved, straggled down my neck.

But he went on, "I have no wish to interrupt your work. I'll just sit here, shall I?"

The old bench had been replaced by a far more comfortable one, close at hand. He sat there, laid his head back, and closed his eyes like a man exhausted—or seeking something. I continued to kneel where I was, trowel in one hand, but the temptation to study him while I had a chance proved irresistible.

How pleasing the lines of his face in repose, how dear to me they had become. I watched as the tension drained out of him, the knot between his brows eased, his jaw relaxed. Oh, how I liked the tiny lines at the corners of his eyes and the way the golden-brown hair spilled over his forehead—the tiny golden hairs on the backs of his hands now folded on his knee.

This day, he wore not the costume of state—indeed, he might have been any ordinary man wearing brown trousers and a plain white shirt he'd opened at the neck. I could see a crop of golden-brown hair there, too, rising and falling with his breaths.

Heat suffused me and I fought it back. I had no right to feel thus about this man. A Prince. I'd spent my life subjugating my feelings. Surely I could continue doing so now.

The quiet of the garden returned. The sunlight shone down, birds fluttered and sang, a butterfly visited the blossoms of the bee balm plants, all in turn. Rupert appeared to doze, and I refrained from disturbing him, wondering a little what heavy troubles he'd put aside to come here today.

My own ease had been restored before he said, "What is it you're doing?"

I looked up to find his gaze resting on me. Steady and green, his eyes appeared to make no judgments, and a faint smile hovered around his lips.

I answered without my usual awkwardness, "I'm transplanting herbs. Donella wanted first to concentrate on the flower beds, but I love herbs, and we saved this plot for them."

"You love herbs?"

"Yes. I used to tend the herb beds back at my father's house."

"Have I been sending you the wrong bouquets all this while? Flowers instead of herbs?"

I sat back on my heels. "Oh, no. I love the flowers you send. Besides, that first bouquet you sent had something fragrant in it—thyme, I think."

"You remember what was in the first bouquet?"

"Of course. I have it still, pressed in one of my books."

The smile lit his entire face. "Why do you like herbs so much?"

"I think because they are so fragrant. I sometimes like to carry a sprig with me just for that reason."

"Ah. Must be why you always smell so good."

He said it casually, yet heat flooded me again. This time, though, I didn't look away from his eyes. I gazed at him and he at me.

"Mistress Bulgar…" he began.

I whispered, "Best to call me Cindra, is it not? If I'm to call you Rupert. Especially here."

"Yes, for it's an enchanted place, isn't it? At least that's how it feels to me when I come. A little bower apart from everything, containing one particularly unique flower."

My eyes widened. "I…"

"You don't know how to take a compliment. I understand. Your brother—well, I hope you don't mind, but he explained a few things to me. Cindra, you don't have to accept my compliments. Please, just let me speak them."

The trowel fell from my fingers. I carefully set down the tiny rosemary plant I held in my other hand. I wanted to run, to hide. I wanted to stay there with him more than anything in the world.

I choked out, "I don't know what Robin told you…"

"Not much. Just why you would find it difficult to accompany me anywhere your mother or sisters might appear. That is why I stopped asking, not because I would not like your company, Cindra. But I would never wish to make you uncomfortable."

"I am always uncomfortable, it seems," I admitted with shame.

"Surely not here, among your plants?"

"Well, no."

"Here you can be you, and I can be me."

Another silence fell. I resumed working, bedding the tiny seedlings into the soil.

"You know," he said then, musing, "I've encountered your mother and your sisters many times. May I be honest with you?"

"Yes."

"Three less appealing women I've rarely met."

My gaze flew to his, startled; my lips parted.

"And," he went on, "I've met women all over the world. Many beautiful women. I've found that what makes them beautiful isn't what's outside but rather what's inside."

"Oh."

"One of the most appealing women I've ever had the privilege of meeting was in the Sultanship of Kreem. She had a scar on her face that ran from here to here." He traced a path from his temple to his cheek.

I continued to gape. "Then how could she be beautiful?"

"She had a beautiful spirit. I would have stayed there with her if I could."

"Oh."

"But I had duties." He smiled ruefully. "And she was wife to another—he who gave her the scar."

"Oh," I said yet again. "If I might ask—"

"You may ask me anything, Cindra. I hope you'll never hesitate, with me."

"What made you wish to stay with her?"

"She had the most wonderful eyes I'd ever seen. Ever seen…up till now."

"Rupert, I am not…"

"Cindra, forgive me for disagreeing, but you cannot see yourself."

"I can. Mirrors—"

"No mirror will show you what I see when I look at you. Your eyes, Cindra, are dark and fathomless as a desert night. They reflect the woman you are—kind and compassionate."

I began to shake my head.

He went on, "I expect you've mistaken your sisters as beautiful."

"Yes." Oh, yes.

"Well, since we're speaking honestly, just the two of us here, I'll confess both of them make my skin crawl."

That I certainly couldn't believe. Men had been chasing my sisters with enthusiasm since they'd made their debuts into society.

But Rupert's brow wrinkled in disgust. "Each of

them, in turn, has thrown herself at me in the most shameless fashion. Bethessa even offered me a sample of her…er…charms ahead of the wedding, as it were."

"And you refused?"

"Good God, do you think I want that in my bed?"

His horror sounded so genuine, it made me laugh. Sudden mirth arose, and I succumbed to it as seldom before; I laughed until I cried.

Rupert laughed with me.

"Oh," I gasped at last, "I would have loved to see Bethessa's face."

"It was a study—insulted and accommodating all at once. Cindra, I like it when you laugh."

"So do I," I admitted.

"Then henceforth, I shall have to make tickling your fancy my life's work."

Chapter Eleven

Rupert came every day after that, usually in late morning. He would come walking down from the castle, dressed just like an ordinary fellow, and sit with me for an hour or so. He always brought me flowers. And frequently he succeeded in making me laugh.

Robin told me later the Prince had built that time into his day—informed his advisors he needed a constitutional. If it rained, he came anyway, arriving with the shoulders of his coat wet and his hair darkened to the color of raw honey. We would sit in the parlor together and play a game he taught me, something he'd picked up during his travels in the East.

Since Robin was usually away at his work and Donella invariably left us, citing household duties, we frequently found ourselves alone, which I suppose was not strictly proper. But I lived for those hours and for the moment when, at parting, Rupert lifted my fingers to his lips. This he did even if they bore a coating of garden soil.

Then he would smile, his green eyes would sparkle, and I'd smile too.

"He's courting you," Donella insisted, though I refused to consider any such thing.

Robin agreed. "He's stopped so much as looking at other women."

Donella ordered me a whole new crop of what she

called "gardening frocks." Simple in design, she chose an assortment of charming prints and blithely told me I must feel free to get them as muddy as I liked.

I began to feel…but I had no words to describe it. Not beautiful, never that, not for all Rupert's subtle compliments. My standard of beauty—if not his—was too high. Perhaps the word *whole* comes closest to describing it: I felt whole in his company.

One morning I went so far as to mention it. The time neared for him to leave and return to the meetings, supplicants, and other demands of his life. We'd been very silly that morning, lounging in the garden, playing games, and laughing at nonsense. Rupert had tucked a bloom in my hair—a yellow nasturtium—and the look in his eyes stole my breath.

I asked in a whisper, "Rupert, are you courting me?"

"I am. Couldn't you tell? I must be doing a damned poor job of it, then."

"Well, I thought—perhaps we were friends."

"We are friends. I'm courting my friend, you see."

"Oh."

"Cindra, I'm no courtier. I have no glib words. But if you could see what's in my heart…"

"I think I can."

"Then please don't doubt me." He rose from the bench where we sat and pulled me up also, by the hand. "Life is not easy right now. I fear what must come. I wish a hundred things were different, but yes, I am most definitely courting you."

He kissed my hand, not the back, as always at leaving, but the palm this time, pressing his lips deep. "There. That is my heart. In your keeping."

My legs trembled beneath me. He pulled me into his arms. For several moments he just held me, our hearts beating against one another. I could smell the warmth of him—so much like sunshine—and I absorbed the exquisite sensation of touching him.

Then I felt his lips at my ear.

"Cindra, may I kiss you?"

My lips parted in surprise. "You're a Prince. And I…"

"I'll take that for a yes."

As our first kiss, it proved astounding. I'd never imagined such warmth, such comfort, such claiming. I'd never imagined, either, the sensations that rushed through me, primal and powerful.

Gently, gently he bestowed the caress. Then we gazed into one another's eyes.

Looking into Rupert's eyes felt like gazing into the sea—wide, deep, and limitless—even though I'd never seen the sea, except for an illustration on the printed page.

"Will you be here for me, Cindra? Here, whenever I can come?"

I nodded. "I promise I will."

****

But he did not come the next day, though a bouquet did arrive, seven tiny, perfect red roses. No note. I did not know what to think until Robin returned home and came straight to me.

"Sister, the King died last night."

"Rupert's father?" The King meant little to me, beyond that.

Robin nodded gravely. "He passed in the wee hours of the morning, just slipped away. It has been much expected, but a heavy burden, for all that."

"Rupert will not be able to get away and come here."

"No. The funeral has been long planned and will take place tomorrow."

Donella came to sit next to me. "Cindra, dear, will you want to attend?"

Horror flooded through me, closely followed by a rush of compassion. Of course I wanted to support Rupert. But…

"Everyone will be there," I whispered.

"Well, that's just it. It's a state funeral—everyone will be there. Even foreign dignitaries are coming."

"Father? Mother?"

Robin looked grim. "Even if she has to drag herself from her bed."

I hesitated. "She's still ill?"

"I suspect it's more a matter of vanity than anything else at this point. Father says she lies in a darkened room all day. But yes, if you go, you'll have to face her. All of them."

I sucked in a breath. Rupert depended on me. He would want me there. How could I let him down? But could I do this impossible thing?

"I think," Robin confirmed, "it would mean a great deal to the Prince, seeing you there."

Rupert pressing his lips—his heart—into my hand. I must show him he hadn't misplaced it.

"Very well. I will accompany the two of you."

Donella immediately snapped to life. "Come, we will select a gown and decide how you should wear your hair. I suspect we can lend you a measure of style."

I doubted it. But I imagined us sitting somewhere near the back, lost in the crowd. If Rupert caught a glimpse of me, it would be enough.

Things did not work out quite that way.

****

On the day of the funeral, Donella dressed me in a gown of purple so deep it looked nearly black, decorated all over with bobbles of jet, and a matching cape. From somewhere she produced a black hat with a brim that tipped up on one side and down on the other, half obscuring my face. Beneath this she twisted my hair, all upswept.

I'd never before worn a hat and found I liked it. I felt concealed, masked, and that allowed me to hold my head higher.

If my face was crooked, at least part of it now also lay hidden.

"You look very well," Donella assured me.

The funeral commenced in late afternoon. Amazingly, flowers arrived that morning—not a bouquet but a little posy in a worked silver clasp that Donella insisted on pinning at my breast.

"There. It matches your gown. And it shows he's thinking of you amid all this madness."

The scale of the madness I never imagined till we arrived at the cathedral. A mass of carriages blocked the road—we could not get near and like hundreds of others had to walk the last of the distance.

For one such as I, unused to appearing in public, the crush of bodies and sheer numbers seemed overwhelming. I shrank close to Robin's side and clutched his arm, but save for a few nods and curious glances, no one paid us much attention. All eyes focused on the cathedral and the figures inside—foreign ministers, even a neighboring King, and of course our royal family, which apparently included a number of Rupert's young cousins.

It must have taken well over an hour to wend our way inside. Between my fear and a general sense of panic, I nearly fainted several times.

We had no sooner reached the back of the nave than a man flagged Robin down.

"Master Bulgar, please to come with me."

Robin shot a desperate look at us, his charges.

The man waved a hand. "You and those with you."

We went. The man guided us through the tight press of bodies, telling us as he led the way, "The Prince bade me watch for you. We have places for special guests up front."

Up front? Oh, no! I tried to draw back, but flight had become doubly impossible. The crowd closed behind us like a brick wall.

Up ahead, though, I saw the bishop, clad all in white, and another member of the clergy—no, two. A number of dignitaries and—oh, there was the Queen, dressed all in black and looking pale enough to swoon. A grand bier holding what must be the King's coffin. And—oh, Rupert!

It seemed so strange seeing him here. All our time together had been spent in the garden—my world. Now we were in his.

The seats that had been saved for us were in the second row back. But before we could reach them, Rupert looked round and saw us.

His face lit. He gestured to us, and Robin changed course immediately. Rupert was, after all, his liege—

and now his King.

That realization hit me in the gut. Yet Rupert's gaze reached for me, full of gladness and what might be relief. He barely glanced at Robin or Donella.

"You came. I scarcely dared hope you would."

He held his hand out to me. Robin passed my fingers into Rupert's possession. Rupert drew me to his side, our palms fused. Robin and Donella went away to their seats.

I stood.

I confess I did not comprehend the significance of Rupert's action then. But he'd claimed me before thousands of eyes—before a kingdom—and kept me at his side on this most significant occasion.

The Queen gave me a startled glance. I doubted, in her extremity, she recognized me as the clumsy maid who'd showered her with jam tarts, but she at least grasped the meaning behind my presence. She raked her son with her gaze but said nothing.

As for me—pinned there before all those eyes—I wanted to fall through the floor of the raised apron where we stood, wanted to turn into mist and dissipate. But Rupert's touch captured and upheld me. His desire for my presence gave me strength enough to straighten my spine and lift my head high, knees locked.

Because I could feel his need—all throughout that endless, formal ceremony while he said farewell to his father and assumed responsibilities I could not even imagine.

And I knew I could no longer, in truth, claim I meant nothing to anyone.

Chapter Twelve

"Everyone is talking about you," Donella told me eagerly the next morning. "Wondering and speculating over the identity of the elegant woman the Prince kept at his side throughout yesterday's service."

Elegant? Surely she must be massaging the truth. I'd managed to stand tall and keep from shaming Rupert by passing out during that long time until he at last released my hand and went to the head of the bier, where he led his father's coffin out of the nave to burial in a vault deep below the castle. I'd lost track of him then, and we'd left for our carriage soon after.

Reaction had truly hit me when I awoke this morning. Now I sat at breakfast with Donella, Robin already having gone to the castle. Wrapped in my shabby robe there, I felt anything but elegant.

Donella poured tea from the pot. "It seems no one recognized you. Not too surprising, really, since you've been more or less retired from the world most of your life—and speculation runs rife."

"How do you know this?"

"No fewer than three friends have stopped by already this morning, folks who saw you with us. I, of course, told them nothing."

I pulled the shawl collar of the robe closer around my throat and shivered a little. I didn't know how I'd managed to endure all those stares yesterday, but I could still feel Rupert's hand pressed to mine.

"Of course"—Donella smiled a little less exuberantly—"your family knows the truth. I suppose they may talk—or brag."

Brag? About me? I shuddered, recalling the terrible moment when, leaving for our carriage, we'd come face to face with them. They'd been in a pew near the back of the cathedral, and I don't know if even they had recognized me before then. Robin, of course, stopped to greet them, and they all turned their eyes on me. Mother…

Mother had looked dreadful, pale and weak, her face mostly hidden behind a black veil. Only her fine clothing seemed the same.

Now, *she* personified elegance.

My father, seeing me, seemed too startled to speak. Both my sisters stared with sharp eyes. Mother swayed where she stood.

Donella had swept me past them, leaving Robin to catch up with us after speaking with Father.

"I daresay," Donella added darkly now, "they never expected this development."

I wanted to ask her opinion of just what had happened yesterday, snag her arm and make her deliberate the significance of Rupert anchoring me to his side that way. But in my heart, I already knew. In that one movement he'd progressed from casual, secret meetings in Donella's garden to a virtual public declaration.

Now people speculated about me. And when they discerned my identity—as surely they must—a whole new humiliation would start. For people would mercilessly examine everything about me, from my limp hair to my misshapen face.

I could not endure that. I wanted to run away—far away—and hide myself in some far country. In a cave, in a tomb.

As I'd hidden all my life.

Donella pushed the tea cup toward me and eyed me speculatively. "Drink. You know, I wouldn't be at all surprised if we hear from your family sooner rather than later. They may even come calling."

"God, no!"

"My money is on your sisters showing up first."

"I will not see them. Donella, say I won't have to."

"You needn't see anyone you don't wish, my dear. It will give me great pleasure to turn them away. What is it Robin says they used to call you?"

"Cinder-Ugly. Because I worked among the cinders in the kitchen and I am…"

"Cows! I wonder what they think now. You know, I believe we need to order you a whole crop of hats. The one you wore yesterday was ever so becoming. It will be part of your style—a hat for every occasion."

"Style? I have no style."

"You most certainly do. Regal, people are saying. Understated elegance."

So understated it didn't actually exist.

"I will send for the milliner directly after breakfast."

We were interrupted at that point by one of the maids, who entered the room bearing a bouquet of flowers, this one large and magnificent. The blooms, all purple, matched the gown I'd worn yesterday, and their heady fragrance preceded them.

"For you, miss."

She set it on the table in front of me. I opened the snowy white envelope set among the stems.

Thank you. I hope to call on you later today. Many demands. Please await me.

That was all—no name. No need for one. My poor heart, struggling in my chest, took flight like an injured bird.

I could not do this thing.

For his sake, I must.

****

He never came till nightfall, when Robin brought him. The two arrived quietly, without fanfare, and Robin escorted him through the house to the garden where I waited.

Robin left him there, and Rupert came to me alone. I got to my feet and met him with hands outstretched.

Donella had insisted on dressing me in one of my finer gowns and twisting my hair up on the back of my head. Now, in the soft dark, I wasn't sure Rupert could see me very clearly. He seized my hands, though, and pulled me directly into his arms. For several moments he just held me, and I felt the tension drain out of him.

"How are you?" I murmured.

"Better. Better now."

And suddenly nothing else mattered—not the staring eyes or the feeling of exposure or the rampant speculation. Only that we stood here together and he wanted to be with me.

He released me at last, put his finger beneath my chin, and tipped my face upward. He gazed into my eyes before he kissed me softly, softly, a quest containing no demand. My heart opened within me. I caught his face between my hands and kissed him in return—a comfort and a pledge.

“My God, what a day,” he groaned. “I feel like the sky has fallen on my head. All I could think about was coming here to be with you.”

“Here—sit.” I pulled him down on the bench. “Would you like some refreshment? Shall I send for the maid?”

He clasped my fingers more tightly. “I have all I need now.”

“How is your mother?”

“Prostrate. She has taken to her bed and refuses to see anyone, not even her maid.”

“I’m so sorry.”

“There are matters of state that must be resolved, documents she must sign. Plus—I do not doubt we will soon be at war.”

“What?”

“Nothing but my father’s presence, and the treaty he had with King Ortis, has kept Ortis from attacking before now. With Father dead, Ortis will declare the treaty broken. You notice, he did not send so much as one representative to the funeral.”

I had not noticed much.

“But—but, war,” I stammered.

“I called up the army early this morning, and I’ve sent runners to outlying areas, advising our folk to come and take refuge in the city. If Ortis attacks, he’ll come with fire, pike, and sword.”

“Surely not.”

Rupert raised our linked fingers and caressed my cheek. “He has already extended his borders northward. The sea lies to the east. And we are a wealthy, if small, plum.”

“Can our army successfully repel him?”

“You want the truth? I don’t know. If it comes to that, it will require every man. Your father. Your brother. Myself included.”

“You?” My heart sank violently. “But you’re the Prin—King!”

“And not the man to send others out to die in my stead. Among the many things I learned away at my education was warfare. I’m prepared, I think.”

I drew a painful breath.

He spoke before I could. “Cindra, I’m so glad I had the hours here with you, in the peace of this place, to carry with me now.” He traced my palm with his finger. “You know you hold my heart. Dare I hope for yours in return?”

I swallowed convulsively before I said, “It is not much of a prize—damaged and shuttered and kept closed far too long.”

“It is as beautiful as this garden, and the one place I want to be.”

“Then I gift it, gladly, into your keeping.”

He kissed me again, and this time I tasted fire along with the devotion.

Ruefully he said, “Among the many matters of state is that of securing the succession. I’ve been harangued by my advisors all morning about what will happen should I fall in battle without leaving an heir.”

“Fall in battle?”

“It will be Ortis’s main goal. With me out of the way, the kingdom will stand defenseless. Oh, there are my cousins, but they’re young and not fit to lead. My advisors say I should wed before I ride out.”

He slid from the bench to the ground, onto his

knees, and still holding my hands. I could no longer see his face clearly for the twilight, but I felt his gaze engage mine.

"Cindra—I have come ill prepared. I have no ring with which to beguile you. In truth, I have little to offer you save duties you likely do not want and a dangerous, uncertain future. But I love you—you must know by now how much I love you. And, war or peace, whatever lies ahead, I want you to be my wife."

"Me?" I gasped. "Me, of all women?"

"Of all women."

"But there are hundreds, thousands better suited."

"Only one I want."

"I'm—I'm not capable. Rupert, I might as well have spent my life in a cloister for all I know of the world or matters of state."

"I know. I know how hard it will be for you. I'm sorry, but I need you. And I hoped—I hoped love might be enough to make you countenance the impossible."

Was it? My heart had never loved. Not till now. And the contents of a lifetime's longing were poised to shower upon him.

But could I face it? The scrutiny, the public appearances, the sneers and the derision?

Was I capable of such self-sacrifice even for him?

Could I refuse? He knelt before me, hands clutching mine so hard it hurt, his gaze imploring.

"Be my strength, Cindra," he whispered. "Be my peace in this world."

And I whispered in return, "I will."

Chapter Thirteen

War broke out on the afternoon of our wedding day. I'd begged for a small, private ceremony and Rupert agreed, saying we could hold a state celebration later when—if—the crisis passed. Now did not seem the proper time for it, with disaster on the horizon and Rupert's father scarcely in his tomb.

We were joined in the cathedral by the bishop, with but three witnesses—Robin, Donella, and the Queen. Somehow, what took place was kept under wraps.

I wore a gown of ivory silk, the same Donella had worn, since we had no time to have one made, and Rupert his dress uniform, the one with all the golden braid. To say truly, I barely noticed.

Rupert told me we'd pose for a wedding portrait later, if we had the opportunity; I could not even imagine it.

Afterward, we retired to the Queen's private rooms in the castle for a meal. There, Rupert found waiting for him a formal declaration of war from King Ortis. He read it in dead silence and snorted bitterly. "So he declares our treaty null and void and gives me the option of peaceful surrender. Surrender!"

He turned and looked at the rest of us, his eyes glowing green as those of an angry cat. "I will show him surrender."

The Queen asked through wooden lips, "What will

you do?"

"First I will go draft a reply to this, and then I will celebrate my wedding night. Tomorrow morning we'll ride out to meet Ortis's army."

Wedding night. I confess, I'd barely let myself go there in my mind.

Rupert came to me. "Forgive me, my darling. I must go to my secretary and take care of this. I will return just as soon as I can."

"I understand."

"Do you? God, I hope so." He turned to Robin, Donella, and his mother in turn. "Please, keep my new wife company. Enjoy your meal. Cindra, those flowers on the table are for you."

He caught my fingers and pressed them to his lips. As swiftly as that, he left me.

****

I did not see my bridegroom again until much later, when he came to our chamber, where I awaited him. The room, an enchanting space situated at the top of the highest tower, offered the privacy I craved, or at least an illusion of it. A warm fire burned and a second supper had been set out on a small table. The four-poster bed had been turned down, but I'd not ventured there. Instead, I paced the circular space on pins and needles.

I wore a gorgeous bed gown with which Donella had presented me, all lilac satin and lace. It failed to make me feel lovely, however, because it revealed far too much—skin and subsequently scars—that I usually kept well hidden. I did not wish Rupert to see them.

He came at last, quietly, and let himself in. He still wore his wedding suit but had lost the jacket somewhere. The collar of his shirt lay open, and his hair stood all on end as if he'd combed it repeatedly with his fingers.

I turned to face him, and my heart lurched. All the breath left me in a rush.

"Thank God! I thought I'd never reach here." He crossed the floor and took me in his arms.

And just like that, it all came right. Whatever else happened, whomever he or I might be, whether or not our world fell apart, I was meant to be with this man.

He kissed me and ran his hands down my back; they trembled. "You look…"

"Do not say 'beautiful.' I'll never believe you."

"Then you'll need to muzzle me this night, and that would be a terrible sin. I have plans for my lips."

I laughed shakily. "Yes?"

"Oh, yes. I doubt a council of war has ever before been held while its leader thought only about disrobing his wife."

"Let me extinguish the lights."

"No."

"Please, Rupert," I begged.

"Cindra, I will not say 'no' to you often. Tonight I must. I will need these memories to take with me when I ride out tomorrow."

"Must it be tomorrow?" I gasped in dismay.

"At first light. And I must do my best to leave you with my child before then. Do you understand what that means?"

"I think so."

"This night, for a few hours, we'll become one. Our hearts will join and our bodies also."

"Our hearts have already joined."

"Yes. So, my Cindra, you will deny me nothing?"

I met his eyes, unflinching. "Nothing. But my body—it is not beautiful." I steeled myself and reached for the ties on my negligee. "I'll show you."

"No, let me. This may be the only opportunity I have to undress my wife."

I surrendered myself to his hands. He removed my bed gown slowly, gently, and with inexpressible tenderness. His lips followed everywhere his fingers went—down my neck, across one shoulder, to my breast.

When he turned me around, he froze. "This…" I heard him choke and knew he'd seen my scars. "Did your mother do this?"

"Yes. Please, now can we put out the lights?"

"Wait." He kissed the scars on my back, the touch of his lips butterfly light. Many of the welts had healed without mark; only those that had cut deepest had left ridges. Feeling his careful caress, I began to weep.

"No." He turned me to face him. "There'll be no tears this night."

"No. No tears." I kissed him and felt some of the pain melt away.

He swept me up and carried me to the bed. What happened thereafter, I cannot bring myself to describe. Except…I'd never imagined such completeness as found me when we became one in truth. Our hearts beat together, and I clung to him and defied him by weeping after all. But for the first time in my life, they were tears of joy.

Whether or not he succeeded in giving me his child during that night, I could not tell. I knew the time flew much too quickly and pain beset me when dawn lighted the sky beyond the tower.

"Husband, do not go. Make the night come over again."

"I would, if I could. I don't want to leave you." He buried his face in my neck and inhaled my scent. "Be brave for me."

Brave. Did he know what he asked? He left me in a public forum, facing the sensation caused by our private wedding, without him at my side. But—but—he went to face something far more terrifying: warfare and the defense of our kingdom. Surely if he had the strength, I must also.

I wound my arms around him. "Promise me something."

"What, love?"

"That you'll return. Whatever happens, you'll come back to me."

He withdrew far enough to gaze into my eyes. I saw agony hone the planes of his face before I heard, "I cannot make that promise, Cindra. I wish that I could. But I was born to spend myself for this kingdom—prepared all my life for it. I never expected to find a woman who—"

"Who?" I prompted, aching.

"Brings such comfort to my soul. All I can promise, love, is that I will move heaven and earth to come back to you—only my death or capture will prevent it."

Death or capture. Panic set my pulse to pounding.

"And," he told me, "I will carry you with me every moment."

"You must return," I told him. "For do I not hold your heart in my hand?"

He made love to me again there in the dawn light, one last time, before we rose and, hand in hand, went out to face the world.

It didn't take long for necessity to break in upon the fragile peace we'd forged. He was almost immediately called away to matters of state and to review the troops, mustered in the square down below the castle. I did not so much as see him again for hours. When I did…

How can I hope to describe that final scene, burned forever into my mind? The plaza overflowed with people—soldiers, Rupert's advisors, and the clergy standing by ready to give a blessing, along with every citizen who could press his or her way close enough to watch the scene.

A very public leave-taking. I stood on the lower terrace at Rupert's side and with Donella at my elbow—I do not think she'd realized Robin would be leaving, also, till he showed up in uniform, looking determined and grim. The Queen stood by, appearing a mere shadow of herself, and Rupert made a speech during which he announced our marriage by introducing me.

"My new wife, Queen Cindra Octavius. I hope you will all love, venerate, and honor her as I do."

Queen. I confess, I had not grasped that detail till he said it. The Queen was the Queen—Dowager Queen now, I supposed. Rupert could not have found anyone more ill-equipped to fill the place.

But he loved me. The truth of that lay in his gaze that caressed me, the lingering touch of his hands on mine—all we were permitted then. I must do as he asked and be strong.

Not for me, but for him.

Yet his dearly loved face and form blurred before my eyes as he moved away and, to the sound of cheering, led his troops—nearly every fit man of the kingdom—away. I stood swaying on my feet, praying I would not fall, with the clatter of their departure all around me. Weapons and voices and horses' hooves on the cobbles. I stood, and everyone with me, till we could see only the dust of their passing on the morning air, and then not even that.

The hush, among so many people, became uncanny. When at last I withdrew my gaze from the far distance, I realized they all looked to me.

To me! Oh, God, oh, God.

I supposed my family must be there somewhere, though I certainly couldn't locate them. My mother. That made it harder when I sucked in a breath and said, "Pray for them."

As if I'd summoned him, the bishop moved forward to my side. I returned to the castle on his arm and heard the citizenry disperse behind me.

I only hoped none could see the dark pit of terror in my soul.

Chapter Fourteen

When flowers were brought to me the next morning, I broke down and wept inconsolably.

I sat at the breakfast table with Donella and the Queen—Dowager Queen—and a young boy came in carrying a posy of yellow blooms with one red rose at its heart.

After I mastered my tears, the lad told me, "My father is the florist in town. The King arranged for us to send a bouquet every day so long as the flowers hold out, Your Majesty."

So long as they hold out. A stark reminder of how our lives would change during wartime. All the things we took for granted, even I who had not lived in luxury, would fade and die just like these blooms.

All except his love.

I thanked the lad, who then ran off. The Dowager looked at me.

"I must confess, Cindra, I did not know what to think when my son decided so precipitously to marry you. But I am glad he has your love now. And I hope you will soon have good news for us."

"I hope so too, Madame." I looked at the flowers and not at her. "I wish only that he—that all of them—might come home soon."

I did not get that wish. At first we received news daily from the front, just as I received flowers. Rupert sent couriers with dispatches over which his ministers pored. Our army had engaged King Ortis almost immediately, on the northwestern border. Fighting was fierce, but they hoped for a swift victory.

I lived for the arrival of those couriers. As long as Rupert continued to send messages, I knew he lived. I lay in our big bed at night, praying for his safety and reliving the short hours we'd shared together. My heart beat for him.

And the time dragged far more slowly than chilled honey flowed.

For all that, Donella's estimation proved correct. It could not have been three days before my family came calling. Father, considered too old to enlist, had stayed back and taken up duties defending the city. My sisters and mother arrived all clothed in their best, a dazzling display of color and elegance. I had rarely seen them got up so fine, and it stunned me that they would prepare so, just to see me.

I received them—as I decided I must—in the comfortable chamber where I and the Dowager Queen often sat, which had begun to feel like my own. I'd only shortly before received a report from two of Rupert's advisors—the dispatches were still spread on the table—when my family was announced.

I hastily gathered up the papers and thrust them back into the leather portfolio—all but one, most precious. Rupert had written me a note in his own hand, and had drawn a tiny flower next to his name. That one I tucked into my bosom.

I rose to my feet when my family came in, pulling my emotions around me like armor. If I could have refused to see them, I would have.

But as Queen, I could not. I'd already received a staggering number of people—tradesmen warning they would soon run out of stock, mothers complaining about the lack of police presence on the street. Mostly I listened. I felt I did so in Rupert's stead.

This encounter felt vastly different. My visitors came not to see Rupert but me.

And I'd forgotten—forgotten in the safety of Rupert's love—just how beautiful my sisters were. They entered wearing those familiar expressions of superiority and with every golden curl in place. Bethessa wore blue and Nelissa pearl satin, perfection down to their tiny slippers.

I might have done well to remind myself they could no longer intimidate me. I was now Queen. In truth, they did still intimidate me, an involuntary response that reached to my bone.

Still, easier to face them than my mother—I could not look at her at all beyond one swift glance that showed me she'd come clad in ruby silk and still wore a veil.

"Cindra," one of my sisters cried, and they both flew at me. Horror at finding myself in their embrace had me stepping backward; I held up a hand.

"Please do not touch me."

They paused, barely an arm's length away, and I added, "Anyway, don't you mean 'Cinder-Ugly'?"

"Do not be that way, Daughter," said Mother. "We've come to make amends."

I did look at her then. Through the veil I could see that her face twisted in rage, and I had a sudden memory of the leather strap rising and falling.

"Amends," I repeated. "Truly?"

"Yes, of course. We are your family."

She tossed the veil back from her face, and I barely kept from gasping. The lovely woman she'd once been no longer existed. Instead her features looked unnatural, the skin too tight. A crescent-shaped scar sat at each temple. She'd arranged her hair artfully in an attempt to conceal them, but my eye became drawn there anyway.

I took all this in with one flicker of a glance and looked away again.

"Ah," she said, "I can see your shock."

You are no longer more beautiful than me. I did not speak the words, though little to my credit I ached to. I wanted to ask her: *How does it feel?*

Instead I waved a hand. "Will you sit?"

They did, scattering among the chairs set close together.

Mother asked peevishly, "Cindra, why did you not send us word that you were to wed?"

I focused on the flowers in the vase on the table beside me—blue delphiniums, today's gift from Rupert. "It was a private ceremony."

"But we're your family," Nelissa protested.

I lifted my eyes to her perfect face and encountered blue eyes bright with something that might be spite. "Are you?"

She shifted in her chair. Before she could speak, Mother rushed in, "Well, certainly. I understand Robin and Donella were there."

She was interrupted at that point by Donella herself, who burst into the room, breathless. Donella's gaze flew to me before she acknowledged her in-laws.

"La! This is unexpected."

Mother replied waspishly, "I fail to see why.

Aren't we expected to visit our daughter and sister—the Queen—and congratulate her on her marriage?"

I saw then precisely why they had come. I heard Mother say again as once she had, *My daughter will be a princess.*

Or a queen. But I did not feel like a queen, and they did not feel like my family.

Bethessa spoke before anyone else could. "It was a terrible slight for you to exclude us."

Donella snorted.

Mother pressed, "The Prince—King—did not even ask our leave for your hand. It isn't proper."

"King Rupert asked Robin's permission," Donella replied, "since Cindra was living beneath our roof. Anyway, she's of age and needs no one's permission."

Bethessa narrowed her eyes. "I think it's suspect. Why, I'm betrothed, and my fiancé spoke to Father first."

I said the only thing I could. "Congratulations."

Bethessa's face crumpled. "He's gone off fighting."

"Which is, in part, what brings us." Mother spoke briskly now. "If the battles go badly, or so we hear, the city is likely to come under attack. This castle will then be the safest place to be. We think you should move us in."

"In? Here?" I squealed.

"Indeed. These walls are defensible. I understand there are supplies in case of siege. And as your family, we deserve special consideration."

I surged to my feet. "I would like you to leave. Now."

"Cindra!" Nelissa breathed.

Mother arose, and we stood facing one another, nearly of a height. “How dare you dismiss me?”

“How dare you sue special favors from me?” I returned, furious. I’m not sure I’d ever before felt anger toward her. Fearful, ashamed, cowed, and humiliated, yes, but angry? No.

Now rage set me to shaking. “You come to me seeking privileges? Shall I offer you the same you offered me beneath your roof?”

Donella touched my arm. “Cindra…”

Mother yanked her chin higher. “Whatever lies between us in the past, we are still your family. And this is a crisis. I should think you’d do what’s right.”

“I shall. With God’s help, I hope to. Our men—those we love—stand in danger. I refuse to countenance the possibility of them falling. But I forget—you don’t know the meaning of love.”

She stepped forward and lifted her hand to strike me. Donella and Nelissa both hurried to intervene.

“No, Mother, it is treason,” Nelissa warned.

Mother’s blue eyes shot sparks. “Ungrateful wretch! Tell me but one thing. How did you entrap him? How trick him into marrying you when my beautiful daughters couldn’t catch his interest?”

With friendship, laughter, and comfort. But I didn’t speak those words. Instead I walked to the door, hauled it open, and called to the nearest footman, an aged fellow brought out of retirement in the absence of the younger servants.

“Please show these guests the door.”

“Cindra,” Bethessa gasped in turn.

I stood at the sitting room window till they went. Then I fell into Donella’s waiting arms and wept.

Chapter Fifteen

We continued to receive sporadic dispatches from the front, which is how we learned the fight went badly. First the loss of one battle, and then another. Our troops slowly gave ground and suffered devastating casualties.

I knew Rupert lived because he sent home messages, written in his own hand, to his advisors. Sometimes these were carried part of the way by ordinary people—old men, women, and once even a child.

Whenever he could, he enclosed a short note to me, often including a drawing of a flower. Real flowers no longer existed in our world—autumn hurried toward winter, and scarcity put an end to his kind gesture.

But not his love. I felt that anew every time his minister put another missive—often stained and torn, and once splashed with blood—into my hand.

My darling Cindra, how I wish I might be with you tonight, to restore myself at your deep well. Pray for us. You hold my heart—R.

Rupert's senior advisor, an old man called Rellison who'd also served Octavius, treated me kindly. We fell into the habit of meeting each time a dispatch came in, at which point he would or would not give me my missive, depending on my fortune. Then he included me in the ensuing discussion of what could or should be done to help our men.

By then, of course, I knew I carried Rupert's child. Our single, enchanted night together had at least achieved its state purpose. I told no one save Donella and my little maid, Gerta, who often caught me in the throes of morning sickness.

Since it remained too dangerous to send messages that might be intercepted to the front, Rupert did not know. I imagined telling him, weaving endless scenarios, and pictured the glad light taking hold in his green eyes.

I let myself think no farther than that moment, would not consider the fact that I—Cinder-Ugly—carried the next ruler of a kingdom. If we still had a kingdom seven months hence.

Chances did not seem good.

Sometimes wounded soldiers returned to the city. Sometimes the dead returned, though that happened far less often. A hospital was set up in the cathedral, and I requested a room should be reserved where the dead could be laid, that their loved ones might come and claim them.

I went there in person whenever I could, on these occasions setting aside my own discomfort. I think it was only then it struck me just how dire things must be for our men on the front. The wounds the dead—and the living, for that matter—bore were most grievous.

I did not want their wives, fathers and mothers, and sometimes children to grieve alone. I stood by and afforded them what time they might need. At the end, most of them bowed to me, or even embraced me.

I didn't realize, on the rainy, windy afternoon another message arrived, that the dead man laid out in the room was my sister Bethessa's betrothed. My family—all four of them—arrived when I did; we stood facing one another just inside the door.

I found myself staring into Bethessa's blue eyes, and my heart fell as I grasped the truth. "I am very sorry," I said.

She brushed past me as if I didn't exist, went to the bier, and studied the young man lying on it.

The rest of them followed. Father alone paused to acknowledge me. "Daughter, it is good of you to do this. It means much."

"What happened to him?" Bethessa asked from the side of the bier.

I stepped to her side and eyed the corpse. He had been a very handsome young man, as might well be expected, with a patrician nose, high, noble forehead, and fair hair now stained with blood. He lay in a tattered uniform that had once been fine, the front of it now slashed like the flesh beneath.

No one answered her—only a fool could fail to see that he'd fought, and fought hard. Scrapes and bruises both old and new marked his skin, and a filthy bandage from an old injury swathed one arm.

Bethessa gazed at him long. Despite my history with her, I felt sympathy, imagining how I might react in her place. By heaven, I would be on my knees at the side of the bier, weeping inconsolably, were that my Rupert.

Yet no tears came to Bethessa's eyes. She merely continued to stand until something inside her appeared to snap.

"Coward!" she snarled at the corpse and slapped him, a nasty little blow that resounded through the silent room. "You were supposed to return to me. Now what am I to do?"

I gasped, and Father caught Bethessa's wrist before she could deliver a second blow.

I saw Mother in her so clearly then: the smallness, the meanness, and the desire to strike out. And I knew my beautiful sister was, in truth, ugly.

Father led Bethessa out. Mother and Nelissa walked past me without a word. Once they were gone, I walked to the corpse, laid my hand on his chest and spoke a prayer.

The next day I learned my father had donned a uniform and left for the front.

He never returned.

****

Winter came hard and early that year, adding to our soldiers' misery. They retreated from our northern border step by step, pursued by Ortis's wolves, who, it was reported, treated our wounded and captured with bloodthirsty brutality.

I lived, now, dispatch by dispatch, eager to learn whether Rupert lived still. No more little notes arrived for me, just desperate messages scrawled in his hand. But every one meant he still drew breath—at least at the time the message had been written.

Uncertainty makes a hard mistress. I think I lost my mind a little during that time. I began dreaming Rupert came to me in the night. We held one another and made love, and when the morning came and I learned it wasn't true, I wept.

But I knew he wanted me to be strong, to put his people—my people—first. So I laid my own terror and insecurity aside and addressed them at the castle, sharing what information I could.

Many women came to me later, kissed my hands, and called me their queen. Forgetting myself completely, I wept with them.

Then came a wave of wounded, the first of them arriving on a frosty morning, with Robin among them. They were laid in the cathedral, and I went among them, sorting the living from the dead. As soon as I saw Robin, I sent for Donella, now heavily pregnant.

Robin reared up from the flagstones and clutched my hand. "Rupert," he said.

I caught my breath. "He lives?"

"He lives. He bade me tell you…" Robin fought for air, and despite my desperation for his message I pushed him down gently. "He says he loves you."

That, among all the messages he might have sent.

Robin struggled on. "Wanted me to tell you…prepare. Get everyone into the castle. There will be a siege."

"Siege?" I repeated stupidly.

"Gather people, supplies. Barricade. He will try and get back in time. If he does not make it…"

My hands flew instinctively to my belly; Robin's gaze followed me. His dark eyes filled with gladness. "Thank God. He'd be so glad to know."

"We may not have a kingdom for his son." The truth of that hit me, perhaps for the first time.

Donella reached us then. She fell to her knees and wept over her husband. "Robin! Oh, my love, where are you hurt? How badly?"

"I've lost my foot, Donella. I'll never be the man you wed."

"I don't care. I don't care!" She kissed him, and I rose and walked to the window, offering them what privacy I could.

Over across the city, snow clouds raced cold as death. I gazed away into the northern distance, whispering only one prayer. *Reach me. Oh, reach me in time*.

Chapter Sixteen

We managed to get nearly everyone inside before the storm hit. Some few refused to come, reluctant to leave their homes and livestock. The aged I ordered brought, carried by their neighbors. Others I deemed free to choose their fates.

Packed to capacity, the castle soon became a place of anxiety, misery, and complaint. Even the Dowager Queen opened her quarters to her friends. Only my room at the top of the tower remained sacrosanct, and that because I hoped when Rupert returned he would use it as a refuge. From there I studied the distances and saw what I thought was smoke, the sign of burning.

I went among our folk, reassuring them and attempting to lend comfort where I might. The gates, I informed them, had been barricaded; the castle remained strong. Only those we admitted would get in.

As the cathedral had been, the castle chapel became our hospital. Robin was taken there, and despite her advanced pregnancy, Donella went with him. I knew it no place for her, but he, soon running a fever, needed the care, and our physicians could not keep up with the onslaught of wounded.

I went every day to see him and speak with the others there, or their kin. I could scarcely believe the condition in which my strong, vibrant brother had returned, and it said more than could anything else about what our men endured at the front. I and Rupert's advisors longed to question him, for he'd been closer to Rupert than anyone. But his fever worsened, and he soon fell to thrashing and raving, unable to tell us anything.

Others in various states of injury did speak. Our men had fought bravely, and the first battles had indeed gone well. All praised Rupert's valor and the strength with which he led them. But King Ortis, so it proved, had hired mercenaries, far northerners, by the look of them, and vastly outnumbered, our men fell back and back.

Thrice, said an earnest boy who spoke with me one frigid afternoon, a livid scar down one cheek, had King Ortis sent terms of surrender. Each time Rupert had returned him a message saying, "We will die first."

"But," the lad said, his blue eyes swimming with tears, "he swore we would not die slaves."

Yet here we were, I thought, packed like herring in a storage container. How long could we endure? Already people asked for food and clean water. Did we but await the end, and subsequent slavery?

Ashamed of the thought in the face of Rupert's great courage, I determined we would stand as strong here as he did out on the field. I gave orders for food to be more strictly rationed, for the children to be schooled in the ballroom, where they could also run and play. I set a session every morning when folk could come to me with their complaints. I might not be able to do anything for them, but they would be heard and would know that I sympathized.

I was besieged during those sessions. Most of those confined to the castle were women, children, and the elderly, in addition to our wounded men. Knowing the value of work for quieting a troubled mind, I set them all to tasks and bade them look out for one another. I also held their hands, and wept and prayed with them. Their terror matched my own.

The wounded, all bearing terrible injuries, died steadily, one or two a day, their numbers increasing as the fever took them. I ordered them carried outside, at first, for burial. Then, when the signs of burning drew closer to the city, I had them removed to the vaults instead. Our exalted dead would have to share room with our fallen.

I worried endlessly about Donella, who refused to leave Robin's side and consequently existed in the vile atmosphere of the hospital. I suggested they withdraw to my chamber, but we feared moving Robin even so short a distance would prove detrimental to him. I lived in terror she would contract the fever he harbored, and thus lose their child.

Already, other women tending their men had fallen ill. For all that, I could scarcely believe no one in my immediate family had been to see Robin. My mother and sisters remained lodged somewhere in the castle, though I'd not seen them. Father had not yet returned from fighting, and I feared for him also. Had he been killed out there somewhere? Did he, with Rupert, fight on, struggling to reach us?

The weather worsened, winter sweeping down early from the north just like the invaders. Most days, when I gazed out from my tower windows, I saw only snow. I despaired that our remaining men would reach us—for all I knew they could be lying out there slaughtered. For no further dispatches arrived. And given the terrible weather, attackers might be at the gates before we saw them.

The castle, a drafty structure at best, could not be kept warm. The number of complaints at my morning sessions increased. Children were falling ill; I commandeered everything that could be used as blanketing, even hangings from the walls. I already knew we had insufficient firewood. Like the rest of our supplies, it dwindled rapidly.

I resolved we'd burn the furniture if we must.

I no longer worried about how Rupert's subjects saw me, how I appeared, or whether or not they thought me ugly. Like everyone else, I went about swaddled in whatever warm clothing I could find, hair braided to get it out of my way, face no longer hidden.

And neither did they seem to notice or care how I looked. My name—Queen Cindra—was on everyone's lips. I dispensed reassurance more than anything else, and once, during a hurried conference, Rellison said to me, "My Queen, I sometimes think *you* are our greatest remaining asset."

God help them all. For I had little to give save compassion.

Then, one frigid morning, I looked up during my morning session and encountered the gaze of my next complainant.

Mother.

The strange thing is I did not at first recognize her. How could I fail to know at once my own mother—even a woman who'd been as distant to me as she?

For the first time since her injury, though, she went without a veil. The surgeon who'd agreed to operate on her—way back when life was still ordinary and such things mattered—had done her no favor. Now, like the rest of us, she'd lost weight. The skin sat ashen on the bones of her face. She'd aged, and for the first time in my life I beheld her with her hair undressed—scraped back severely, sparing her nothing.

Only her eyes looked the same, cold and demanding. Those, I recognized.

A sick feeling churned my gut. I experienced it often and feared for the little one struggling to grow there. But now it nearly prostrated me.

I sat at the table where I always received complainants—no thrones here, and anyway the reception room held dozens of families. She'd waited till the crowd thinned. We were very nearly alone.

"Cindra," she said.

The sound of that voice after so long triggered something in me. I experienced a flashback to that morning when she came to my room on the third floor of Father's house with hate in her eyes and raised the strap again and again.

I shuddered and laced my fingers together. "Madame," I returned.

Her eyebrow twitched. Did she grasp she could expect no special treatment? I'd told her so, the last time she came to me.

She said, "Your sister is ill."

"My sister?"

"Bethessa."

"Many people are ill, Madame."

"She pines for her lost fiancé."

"The same whom she struck and called 'coward'?"

"Emotions run high. Your sisters have both always been sensitive."

To their own feelings, perhaps. “Madame Bulgar, what do you want?”

“Will you not call me ‘Mother’?”

My eyes met hers and—for one of the few times in my life—held. “No.”

“I suppose you wish to keep things formal and avoid accusations of favoritism. I understand that. But something must be done; we are cold. We need more fuel.”

“Where are you being housed?”

Her features twisted with repugnance. “Near the kitchens.”

“You are fortunate. The kitchens emit warmth.”

“We are in a dark, tiny closet. There is no heat from the kitchens or anywhere else.” Her annoyance threatened to overtake her, conciliation never her ready asset.

“No one is comfortable,” I reminded her, “least of all our soldiers. This is war.”

“I’ll warrant you’re comfortable, up in that luxurious room of yours in the tower. I demand you move us in with you for the duration.”

“You demand?”

“It’s the least you owe us.”

“Owe?” I got to my feet as if drawn by ropes. For one telling moment, her eyes dropped to the swell of my belly—Rupert’s child showing now.

Her lip lifted in a sneer. She’d never looked less lovely. “Yes, you think you’re riding high now, don’t you? Carrying the next ruler. But ruler of what? Have you thought about that?”

“Yes.”

“Do you know what Ortis will do to that child if he

seizes this castle?"

"Yes—exactly what you wanted to do to me when I was born."

"I should have, for all the good you're doing me now."

"Madame, please get out of my sight."

"I beg your pardon?"

Emotions rose inside me. I had feared this woman all my life. But since escaping the walled prison of her hatred, I'd learned a few things. Hate did not lend strength but stole it. Compassion, in many cases, made it possible to endure the impossible. I was not sure, given all she had done to me in the past, that I could summon compassion toward my mother. But knowing I could overmaster the hate that beset her gave me a rush—one of the most powerful moments I'd ever known.

I raised my voice, assuming that tone I used only as Queen; everyone left in the room turned to stare. "No one within these walls, Madame, is deserving of special treatment. We all flourish or starve, live or die, together. Now please get back to your assigned place, unless you'd rather be cast outside."

She hissed, and her eyes narrowed like those of a snake. "You wouldn't dare."

I leaned toward her across the table. "Try me, Madame Bulgar."

She left in a huff and never saw the tears in my eyes.

Chapter Seventeen

I regretted it the next day, of course, following a sleepless night. I would not have raised my voice to any other of Rupert's subjects, and in the end, beyond being my mother, she was first and foremost his subject.

I sent Gerta to inquire as to their situation and whether Bethessa needed removing to the hospital. She came back saying they were no worse off than anyone else and better than some, having brought a number of their fine possessions with them, none of which they consented to share.

In Gerta's opinion, which I valued, Bethessa seemed far too ornery to be genuinely ill. I tried to dismiss them from my mind after that but had difficulty. None of them had yet been to see Robin, even once.

That very afternoon the weather cleared, and I climbed the steps to the tower, hoping to see what lay around us.

To the south and as far east as the sea—all our land—everything slept beneath a blanket of white. To the west the rolling hills, blue and white in the distance, stretched to the neighboring kingdom of Khett. To the north…

Devastation. Everything lay burnt and torn and plowed as if a giant boar had raged across it. The horror of the blackened scene hit me in waves, just as the ruin lapped against the edge of the city.

And there—*there…*

Two forces, one great and one small. I blinked as my eyes refused to believe what they saw, and blinked again. A straggling line of dark figures made its way through the now-deserted streets of the town, like a short chain threatening to fail. Pursuing them came a moving blot on the horizon, appearing amorphous and almost harmless from my high perspective.

Ortis's army.

A scream rose to my throat. Wildly, I judged the speed of the two parties and the distance between them. Would our men—what remained of them—make it to the safety of the castle in time?

I screeched like a blackbird and ran. Still wailing, I went down the tower steps at a speed that might well have tripped me up with grave consequences for Rupert's child. I steamed through corridors, telling everyone I passed, "They come. They come!"

I picked up a tail of others as I went. Behind me I heard their voices and cries of, "Queen! Queen!" By the time I pelted through the bailey and reached the gates, I could not speak.

Rellison happened to be there, consulting with the guards. He eyed me in alarm.

"Your Majesty! I was just saying that perhaps we should take advantage of this break in the weather—"

"Open the gates. Open the gates!" I whooped.

"Precisely. There are three more dead…"

"They come!"

"The dead, Majesty?"

I hoped not. Oh, how I hoped not. I looked him in the eye. "Our army. What's left of it."

Glad cries sounded all around me. Rellison and the guards jumped into action.

"Open." Rellison nodded to those manning the gates. "But, Majesty, are they pursued? Is it safe?"

"Ortis's forces are hard after them." I turned to the guards who stared at me. "You will need to be quick and clever. How fast can you raise and lower the portcullis?"

"Fast," said Edward, the head guard. I'd heard he had been a fierce warrior in his day. "Majesty, you are certain?"

"I saw them from the tower. But I could not tell who…" My throat closed.

"Back! Back, everyone! We open the gates!" Edward added to me apologetically, "You too, Majesty. I would take no chances with your safety."

"If you think I am budging from this spot," I told him, "you are mad."

He grinned at me and turned to his work.

"My Queen," Rellison asked, "how long before our men reach us? Could you tell?"

I tried to calculate swiftly. "They have just entered the northern edge of the city."

Edward said, "They may have wounded with them. Should we send men out to meet them, that they might move more swiftly?"

Dangerous. I calculated it with as much dispassion as I could muster. Rupert might not be with them. He might have been captured; he might have perished.

No.

But these, the very men who'd stood with him through the bitter defense of the kingdom, now ran like exhausted hares before fierce hawks.

"Yes." I and Rellison spoke at the same time. Edward bellowed to several of his men. "Who wants to volunteer? I'll send no one against his will on such a mission."

Five of our bravest—all aged, like Edward himself—stepped up. We opened the gates, and they ran.

****

Even now, emotion swamps me when I describe what happened next. The story—the one that's been told and retold—never includes this part. It's all about coaches and grand balls and a magical transference into beauty. It skips right over the war and the siege and how our men returned to us, broken.

But they did return, at least some of them. Bloodied, beyond exhausted, and so changed that, once again, I barely recognized them.

Even my husband.

Uniforms in tatters, wearing filthy bandages as much as anything else, they limped in, assisted by those we'd sent out to them, as well as others who flooded out from the castle in an unstoppable wave. Of the strong force we'd sent out at the beginning of autumn, fewer than fifty returned. I did not at first know the man who came at the front of them, half his face swaddled in bandages stiff with blood, clad in rags, and with his head shaved. God help me, I recognized his voice, giving orders.

"Get everyone inside. Leave no one behind! Shut the gates. Is that everyone? Certain? Shut them. Shut! Bar them!"

"Rupert? Oh, God, oh, God—"

He failed to hear me amid the hollering and

confusion. People still streamed in from all over the castle. The newly arrived were collapsing where they stood. Someone called for the medics, and I moved forward like a woman in a dream, driven to get closer.

People parted for me, bless them. They bowed, and a few called, “Sire!”

I called out also. “Husband!”

That, he heard. He turned, saw me, and froze. I will remember that moment until I die—the staggering relief and gladness of it, which very nearly took me to my knees. Oh, my heart wanted to break for him, seeing the exhaustion in his face, the expression in his one uncovered green eye, and the weight that sat visibly on him.

But none of that mattered. He had come, come, come.

I flew forward straight into his arms. They opened to catch hold of me, and for a moment I knew only bliss—pure gladness at the feel of him, the gift of his presence, the impossible wonder of his return when so many women’s husbands hadn’t come home and never would.

Only after that first wave of joy did other truths become apparent. He stank, and the body beneath the tattered uniform felt like a rack of bones.

I drew back far enough to question him with my gaze. He returned my look gravely and with so much love it stole my breath. His hand flew to cup my cheek and then moved, slowly and with wonder, to hover over the gentle swell of my belly.

“Cindra, never say…”

“Your child, Husband. Your child and heir.”

He kissed me there in front of everyone, a kiss of

need and yearning, of pledging and gratitude. His subjects might have reacted in a number of ways. They cheered mightily, and I wept.

Rellison stepped forward to say, “Your Highness, we give great thanks at your return. Your wife the Queen has been a shining light to everyone in your absence.”

To my astonishment, another cheer arose from the onlookers.

Rupert said, “I am not surprised. My wife is a star in the heavens, one that helped steer me home. But we are hard pursued. It grieves me to tell you, my beloved people, we have all but lost this fight. Ortis set us a trap on our own border and called in mercenaries to fight us. I’m afraid we never stood a chance against so vast a horde. But our men fought bravely and without thought to themselves. Heroes, every one. Now we are faced with two choices: siege or surrender. Which shall we choose?”

“Siege,” I whispered.

All those including Rupert’s battered troops took up the word.

“Siege.”

“Siege!”

“Siege.”

And someone said, “If our valiant Queen can endure it, so can we.”

Chapter Eighteen

Not till many hours later did I have a chance to be alone with my husband. It didn't matter that there were a thousand details to which he must attend. It satisfied me just to have his voice in my ears as he gave orders and spoke with all who came to him. I delighted over and over again in the fact that I could see him, and touch him if I chose.

He breathed, he reached for my hand. He lived.

Being Rupert, he saw to everyone else's needs before his own. His men were, without exception, shown to the chapel to be seen by physicians. All hands were pressed into service bringing hot water and swiftly scrounged bandaging. Questions ran rife.

As did the delivery of bad news. Many of our dead had not been brought back and lay where they'd fallen. Some few had been captured by the enemy. The tales of brave sacrifice abounded.

Rupert broke the news personally when he could. I remained at his side and wondered what kept him on his feet. He seemed so terribly depleted. But he reached often for my hand and more than once touched my belly reverently.

I sat through an eye-opening meeting while he briefed Rellison and others of his advisors. By then, Ortis's army had reached the city. They would soon be at the gates.

Full dark fell before Rellison said, "My King, may I suggest that now, before the siege begins in earnest, you have your own wounds tended? And perhaps take some refreshment." The old man glanced at me. "Alone, perhaps, with your wife."

Rupert smiled ruefully. "I'm not at all certain I can climb so far as the tower."

"Then another chamber can be prepared."

Several among the advisors promptly offered their own.

"Please, Rupert," I begged. I did—and didn't—want to see what lay beneath those dreadful bandages.

"Take my chamber, please, Your Highness," Rellison implored. "I share with several others, but we will busy ourselves here for the time."

In the end, Rupert agreed. When it came time to remove to Rellison's chamber, however, he could not stand. I and two others helped him walk to the small room, where hot water and food were soon brought and a physician sent for.

The physician—the same who had labored over Robin—and I thereafter worked together, and I struggled all the while to keep from weeping.

Beneath his rags and bandages, my husband had wasted to nothing. Every rib showed, and I counted twelve wounds, great and small, some of them months old. The worst were to his leg—I do not know how he walked upon it—and to the left side of his head, where a deep cut lay close beside his eye.

The physician, examining that, asked, "Majesty, can you see?"

"Yes," Rupert replied and, God help me, I could not tell if he lied.

"Sleep," the physician ordered in parting. "It is the medicine you need most desperately."

Rupert nodded.

"We will not have long," he told me when we were at last alone. "The castle will be surrounded by morning."

"Sleep." I repeated the physician. Already Rupert lay stretched on Rellison's bed.

"Lie with me."

"I will, gladly."

We lay together, I with my arms wound closely around him. I could feel his ribs sharp beneath my fingers—I could also feel his heart beating low but steady.

I began to weep. "Oh, Rupert, I can scarcely believe you're here, that you came back to me. I was so afraid."

"Hush, Cindra. You drew me back like a lodestone draws iron."

"What happened to your poor hair?"

"Lice, I'm afraid. It was the only remedy. In fact, I probably still have them…"

"I don't care."

"Fleas too."

"I don't care," I reiterated and kissed him softly. The tears started again.

"Don't weep, my wonderful, miraculous wife."

He once more splayed his fingers on my belly. "You carry my child. And our people love you. *Love you*. As much as I do. Did you hear them, back there?"

"Yes." My mind whirled. "I did only what I could for them."

"You stood strong, as I knew in my heart you

would. Cindra…" He sucked in a breath. "You do know we are likely to go down to defeat."

"No."

"We can endure a siege for a time. Likely we will not hold out till spring. We have too little of anything—food, water, fuel."

"We can fight back."

"With what?"

"Arrows. Boiling water. Stones."

"We will soon run out."

I rose on my elbow and looked at him. "You only say that because you are tired, disheartened. We will not quit."

He smiled sadly and touched my cheek. "Do you know how beautiful you are?"

"I am not…"

"Hush. Yes, you are. Beautiful. I dreamed of your eyes—deep as the night sky. I felt your kiss. Tasted your breasts. You are what kept me alive."

"Oh, Rupert, I'm glad. So glad—"

"I kept thinking if only I could reach you, all would come right, as it used to in your garden, where the world fell away. But, Cindra, the world won't fall away this time. It's all around us. We're trapped here. Rats in a cage. How can I tell my people that? How tell them we're going to die?"

"We are not," I declared, even though I knew very well how strapped for supplies we were, how difficult life had been even before we absorbed another fifty men. "We will share and ration and live on less if we must. But we will live."

Rupert smiled at my words but closed his eyes for a moment like a man in pain before he asked, "How fares your brother?"

"Robin? Well, the poison at the site of his amputated foot has refused to subside. The physicians thought they would need to remove his leg." I left out the fact that Robin now battled fever.

"And Donella?"

"Nearly ready to deliver their child."

Any trace of a smile fled Rupert's face. "Born to this."

"Into the arms of love. Now sleep while you can."

"Only if you kiss me again."

And I did.

He slept with his shaven head on my shoulder, his hand resting over our child—a few short hours' respite only, if it could be called that. He twitched and groaned and cried out in pain. All too soon, Rellison came to the door.

"Forgive me, Majesty. Daylight has come. We are surrounded."

Rupert struggled up—only Rellison and I saw what it cost him. I wanted to weep for his courage but would not insult him with tears. His ruined body hidden beneath clean clothing, he went out to face the impossible.

I went at his side, determined he would not stand alone.

Panic beset the castle. Everyone had seen what now lay beyond the walls—a seething sea of men and horses.

"They will build siege engines," Rupert said.

I told him, "We will destroy them."

"They will pick apart our city and fire the rubble at us."

"We will endure."

Rupert addressed his subjects, pulling no punches. "We stand together, but we stand confined. If we are to outlast our attackers, it will require sacrifices. We have a well in the depths of the castle—I hope it will supply sufficient water. Food will be strictly rationed, as will fuel. We must all help one another, share and share alike. We are now one family."

They received his words in silence, save for weeping. No one voiced the protests sounding in my mind—we had already rationed the food, and fuel stores lay dangerously low. They could see to what their King had been reduced. They saw the way his fingers clung to mine.

The Dowager Queen, a mere shadow of her former self, stood beside him. It was she who asked, "And, when spring comes?"

Rupert lifted his head. "Spring means rebirth. It means new life. It means hope. We will not think beyond that."

In the spring, our child would be born. When first I'd known I carried his heir, I'd worried it might be born like me—misshapen and ugly. Now I worried it would be born to slavery.

"Pray," Rupert bade his people. "And fight with your every breath. Remember, to endure is to fight."

Chapter Nineteen

"I want you to be in charge of rationing," Rupert told me. "It will have to be carefully done, but I know you'll be merciful and fair."

I sighed. I'd been struggling for months with the necessity for rationing but knew we would now need to knuckle down severely.

"I think measures should be maintained for the children," I said, "and the nursing mothers."

"Have we many nursing mothers?"

"No."

"What about expectant mothers?" We were alone in our—Rellison's—chamber, and he caressed the swell of his child gently.

"We can endure. I would not be accused of self-serving or favoritism."

"You may have my portion." His kissed me, and I ached for him, all of him, the way I had in the night when he lay far from me. But we had no time to share ourselves with one another now.

King Ortis's troops ringed the castle on all sides, and Rupert expected him to send a demand for surrender at any time.

"It is a dance in which we have engaged many times during this fight," he told me. "Ortis offers terms for surrender—I refuse. We fall back and back. Now we have retreated as far as we can."

"But we are not vanquished," I reminded him. I knew the depths to which one could fall and the strength in endurance.

"If we do not surrender, the true hardship will begin. Ortis will batter these walls. We will have nothing but our lives."

He was interrupted at that point when the door of the chamber flew open. Donella stood there gasping for breath, her face white as paste, her black hair straggling loose down her back.

For an instant I believed her to be in labor and I flew to her, exclaiming, "For pity's sake! What are you doing on your feet?"

She sagged into my arms, eyes reaching for mine. "It's Robin. I think—I think he's dying."

I flew and Rupert behind me, all else forgotten for the instant. Through crowded corridors where people slept, past those who called to us, and into the chapel that, to me, now always smelled of death. Robin occupied a corner. One of the physicians remained with him when we arrived.

Robin already looked dead. His pallet lay on the cold stone floor, and I dropped to my knees beside him. Donella came down also, heavily.

"Your Majesty," the physician murmured, "I fear—I fear it is not good."

I gazed into the man's eyes; he looked exhausted, but I saw what I did not wish to see, deep regret.

"No," I said. This was Robin, my brother, the one member of my family who'd accepted me, had taken me in.

"I believe," said the physician, "the poison from his leg has reached his brain. It's a slow and inevitable death."

Donella clutched Robin's hands and began to weep. "No! Husband, awake. Awake and stay with me and our child!"

"Send for my mother and sisters," I bade Rupert over my shoulder, and told him where in the castle they lodged. Father had not returned with the rest of our men—we were so few. It seemed no time to let anger get in the way.

He nodded and hurried off. I relieved Donella of one of my brother's hands.

"Robin—please!"

His eyelids did not so much as twitch. I knelt there while Donella poured out her heart to him, told him she could not live without him, begged him to fight on. Rupert returned, having sent a messenger for my mother and sisters.

They never came. Robin died less than an hour later, with Donella sobbing over him.

How can I describe my grief? It filled me to overflowing. But when I staggered to my feet in that terrible place, I found anger overweighed it. I felt outrage at this loss, the unfairness of it. Outrage at Ortis and the slavering mercenary-hounds who'd joined forces with him. Outrage at the death of Robin and Donella's innocent happiness, snatched from them. Outrage at my mother, who could not be bothered to come to her only son before he died.

That, I think, most of all.

Rupert embraced me and Donella, told her we and all the royal family would be there for her. Then he had to leave, needed at the gates, where Ortis, as expected, presented his demands. I wondered how to console

Donella when I also felt inconsolable. I helped her up from Robin's side, and she collapsed again, all her strength gone.

She clung to me and sobbed. "I want to die also! I want to follow him."

"No, my darling—your child needs you. We need you. My dearest friend…"

I don't think she heard me. It took me and two physicians to persuade her away from Robin's corpse. He had to be prepared for burial and taken to the crypts. At last the Dowager Queen arrived and urged Donella away with her own hands to the Queen's chamber, where she might take a strengthening cup of tea from the Queen's store.

Donella went into labor that same afternoon, whilst still Rupert negotiated with our mortal enemy through the barred gates. I cannot say I was surprised, her emotional state being what it was.

A difficult birth. The child presented breech, and Donella needed to fight hard. I gave her what little I could—a hand to hold and every encouraging word I could dredge up from my mind. My nephew was born just as Ortis and his troops began to bombard the castle, a terrifying harbinger of things to come.

Donella, blinded by grief, looked at her child, but I do not think she truly saw him. I sat holding him, gazing down at the tiny mite in my hands, in stunned grief. Rather than Robin's child, he might have been my own. At first I thought his curious form a result of the hard delivery—his right shoulder had snagged in the birth canal a long time. But his small body looked misshapen, with a hump on one side, and the crooked structure of his face echoed my own.

"Oh, little one, little one," I whispered to him. "I am sorry."

I was relieved then, so relieved that Mother had not come. She would have spat and disowned him, said hateful things. I swaddled the child, who did not cry but looked at me gravely, and tucked him into Donella's arms.

"Your son." My brother's son. "What will you call him?"

Donella did not respond. Exhausted by her travail, her eyes sagged shut. Grief touched me again; I wondered how this could be the same lighthearted and generous girl with whom I'd shared laughter in a sunny, summer garden.

Gone, gone.

I sat and wept silently for all of us.

****

Donella left us in the wee hours of the next morning, slipping away in silence to follow her love, while the bombardment of the walls continued like some vile torture. Summoned to her side from my bed, where Rupert had failed to join me, I took my nephew in my arms and stood, too grieved to weep any more tears. To my surprise, I found the Dowager Queen at my side.

I stared at her. She'd come in her nightclothes, with her hair, the color of Rupert's, hanging loose down her back.

"Your Majesty, you should be asleep."

"Who can sleep through this hellish pounding? Oh, my dear, I am so sorry."

She took me in her arms, infant and all. I stiffened in shock, never having experienced a mother's love.

But after a moment I relaxed into her.

The tears did come then. "What am I to do?" I wailed.

"Care for the child."

"What are *we* to do?"

"Keep on. Keep strong."

"What if he does not live? And look—look." I unwrapped my nephew and showed the Dowager his little body. Eyes swimming with tears, she smiled at me.

"It seems he has landed in the perfect hands."

Chapter Twenty

My brother and his wife were laid together in one tomb, closely entwined. I named my nephew Robin and went at once to search out a wet nurse for him.

Curious that Rupert and I had just discussed nursing mothers; we had but a few. The first refused without even glancing at the child in my arms, saying she already had all she could handle. The second, the widow of a soldier, with a child only two months old, paused and considered it.

"Best let me show you," I said. As I had for the Dowager, I unwrapped little Robin and displayed him.

Markka, for such was her name, looked at him long, and then eyed me thoughtfully. She did not say what must be in her mind—*he's like you*—but bit her lip and eventually nodded.

"All right. I'll have him."

"Thank you. I can arrange for extra rations to help keep you in milk."

"That would be welcome, Majesty. We're all starving. And, Majesty, that pounding! I've had no sleep."

"I know," I agreed unhappily.

Her blue eyes met mine. "But this isn't the worst of it, I'll bet. Just the beginning, right?"

"I'm afraid so."

I placed my nephew in her arms.

"He might not make it," she warned me. "He is so very weak."

"I know. I've named him Robin after his father."

"If he lives, Majesty, will you raise him then?"

"Yes." Oh, yes.

"I'm sorry for your grief."

I embraced her. To my surprise, she clutched me back heartily, her arms uniting both me and little Robin. "I'm that glad," she whispered, "to be able to do this, Majesty—for *you*."

A short time after seeing Robin settled, I went to the gates, where Rupert had stationed himself. I wanted to tell him about the child, but the sight that met my eyes stole my breath.

More snow had fallen. It blanketed the town in white, but around the castle, ringing it, Ortis's army made a dark blot, like that of corruption. So many of them. The sun had not long risen on another gray morning, and I blinked in consternation while a single thought entered my mind.

We are all going to die. Markka, Robin, Mother, my sisters—all of us. Donella had merely gone ahead.

Rupert, who looked far too unwell to be on his feet, turned to me. "You should not be here." But he drew me to his side and touched my belly in a fleeting caress.

My eyes narrowed. "We are most definitely trapped."

He smiled wryly and gently reminded me, "It is the nature of a siege."

"What are they doing?" The small black figures outside ran everywhere, industrious as ants.

"Preparing to destroy us. That group there constructs siege engines. Those men over there, ladders.

The ladders are a fool's game, too easily shoved away from the walls." He sounded almost dispassionate. I wondered if I heard exhaustion speaking. "In this group here, you see King Ortis himself. See? The man with the red beard."

"What is he doing?"

"Planning. Scheming. Supposing he has won."

I drew a breath. "Has he?"

Rupert turned his head and looked at me, his injured eye narrowed in a squint, the other clear green. "No, love. Not by half. We have been picking them off with arrows. Right, Tom?" He directed this at the man beside us.

"Right, sire."

"We have men all along the battlements doing that."

"But…" So many targets.

"And we have every hand available making more arrows."

"We will soon run out of wood. Then what?"

"Make them from furniture if we have to. We are not done. Tell her, Tom."

The aged bowman beside him grinned. "Aye, sire, we are not done."

"Our greatest ally is the weather. The cold that pinches us here will ride roughshod over Ortis's troops. They may take frostbite. They may fall ill. They might desert and run home. Do not lose heart. Right, lads?"

Tom responded with another wide smile, and verbal reassurance came from down the line. All the soldiers, some little more than youths, assured me, "Aye, my Queen, take heart!"

I wished I could.

****

"I want to see my grandson."

I turned, startled, when the imperious voice rang through the crowded room.

Markka, Robin, and I stood together in the big chamber, formerly the ballroom, that now housed women—mostly widows—who had young children. The women chattered while the children, like those everywhere, squealed, cried, and played tag throughout the crowded space.

All fell silent, though, when my mother, with my sisters at her back, progressed toward us.

She had her gaze fixed on me to the exclusion of all else. I'd just been cooing over Robin, who lay in Markka's arms while her neighbor held her little daughter, Dinnie. I froze, my finger still extended and breath flooding my lungs.

Anger followed swiftly, and I drew myself up, refusing to dodge her stare. I waited for her to reach us before I said, "Ah, Madame, now you come?"

She bridled. She looked terrible, shockingly so, wrapped in a blanket against the all-pervading chill. Only her head lay bare. Like nearly everyone else, she'd had to cut her hair, the lice being a plague, and nothing softened the scars left from her surgery. Her blue eyes burned like coals stuck into the mask of a scarecrow.

In that moment I didn't care who listened—Markka, so close at my side, or all the other women, most of whom had suffered terrible loss. What was in my heart needed to come out.

"Where were you?" I asked. "Where, when your son died? When your daughter-in-law died? When he"—I gestured at Robin—"was born?"

She stopped as if I'd struck her; I suppose in a way I had. "I am here now." She lifted her head regally. "Show him to me."

I did not respond, wanting nothing so much as to protect the child in Markka's arms from this woman's stare, from her cruelty and condemnation. I wanted to wrap him more tightly in his swaddling, hold him to my breast, hide him.

I knew I could not.

I shot a look at my sisters, neither of whom appeared well, before focusing on Mother again. "He is in my care."

She snorted. "I will take him if I wish."

"You will not. Anyway"—I felt my lip curl—"you will not want him." I steeled myself. "Show her," I told Markka.

You could have heard an eyelash drop in that room. Even the children fell silent.

After shooting me a startled look, Markka uncovered the child in her arms and gently held him up. Robin gave a little squeak as the cold air found him, and I took him from Markka, covered him again, and cuddled him against my shoulder.

A single glimpse had been enough for Mother. Now it was her lip that curled.

Very clearly she cried, "Ah! It is our curse. We will all die!"

Stunned—though I suppose I shouldn't have been—I covered Robin's ear with my hand.

Markka straightened and declared, like a vengeance, "You are wrong, Madame. If the child proves anything like the Queen, he is our strength and our blessing! We could only pray for another such as she."

A murmur traveled through the room. "Our Queen, our Queen!"

Mother's gaze stabbed at me before she glared at my sisters, both silent. She then eyed the room full of women and spat, "Keep him. He is no grandson of mine."

She turned and swept out the way she'd come, women snatching their children out of her path as if her skirts carried a contagion.

That night, when Rupert managed a brief visit to our room at the top of the tower, I related the scene to him.

Resting his head against the back of a chair, eyes closed, he said nothing, though the corners of his mouth tightened.

I paced in front of him. "Rupert—what if our child is born like poor Robin?"

"Then…" Rupert opened his eyes. "We will love her, or him."

"But this child will be heir to a kingdom."

"True."

"I could not bear…"

He stretched out a hand to me. "Come here."

I sat on his knees, and he cuddled me close, my head tucked under his chin. "Do you not love wee Robin?"

"Yes, oh, yes. But that's because I understand—"

"I believe Markka is right. You are our blessing—our secret weapon, if you will. Can you not see how the people adore you? On every side they speak of you to me with warmth, telling of your kindness, your strength and encouragement while I was away. My own mother came to see me."

"The Queen?"

"She admitted she did not know what to expect when I chose you for my wife. She also admitted she now understands what I saw in you. Stellar, I believe she called you. A beautiful choice."

"Beautiful?" I would never get used to hearing that word applied to me.

"Cindra, do you not yet see that all real beauty lies in the spirit? Yours shines from you. I saw that in Donella's garden; I see it still."

"Our child will be beautiful."

"Oh, yes."

Chapter Twenty-One

"Come with me. I wish to show you something."

The Dowager Queen took me by the hand and pulled me away from my charges, a group of children I'd been helping to school. To them she said, "The Queen will be back in a little while."

I looked at Rupert's mother. "What is it, Madame?"

"Hush. I cannot tell you yet. This is for your ears alone. If anyone asks, we go to pay our respects to your brother and his wife, in the crypts."

Completely bewildered, I obeyed. I rarely saw the Dowager so intent as this.

Nearly a month had passed since the siege began. Every day, it seemed, we suffered some loss or endured some new deprivation. All the walls had been damaged, and repaired as best as possible. Food supplies ran dangerously low, but by the grace of God, the well proved plentiful and we had sufficient water.

One could subsist on water and very little else, for a time.

Our men continued to fight from the battlements, often joined now by certain of the women. They fought with bows and arrows, with chunks of stone, and with anything else that came to hand—anything that couldn't be eaten and wouldn't burn. They fought with boiling water and flaming pitch. They destroyed every siege ladder laid against the walls, sometimes at cost of life.

A single mindset, encouraged by Rupert, possessed us all: Do not give in.

As an ally—our only ally—the weather proved all I could have asked. Blast after winter blast of frigid air screamed down from the north, bringing snow and ice. The shelters Ortis's forces erected for themselves blew down, and in the rare intervals when the weather did clear sufficiently that I could look out from the tower, I saw their numbers had shrunk.

"We do not make a rich enough prize to keep the mercenaries interested," Rupert declared to me and his advisors. "We're winning. Now it's just him and us."

We had hope, or so I repeatedly told myself.

I missed Donella, my first friend, sorely. But Markka and I grew closer over Robin's care, and I realized she'd become a friend of sorts. Despite the fact that I was Queen and she the widow of a carter-turned-soldier, we were united as women sharing hardship. By extension, I also became connected to her friends.

And now the Dowager Queen took me by the hand, as a mother might. What could I do but follow?

"Do we not go to pay our respects?" I asked her when we reached the lower levels, where only some priests and the crypt keeper lived. We could have used the space, but the air here remained dank and cold. I shivered as I looked at the Dowager.

"Of course. I come here often to speak with my husband, Rupert's father." She stared at me, her eyes a paler green than Rupert's. "He gives me advice."

"I see."

She smiled. "You think I've gone mad. I have not. I understand he is dead and in the tomb. But I can still hear him."

Grief, I thought, was a curious thing. To what extremes might I not go, had I lost Rupert?

I whispered, "What has he told you?"

"You will see. I know I can trust you."

"Yes."

She led me on past the grand tombs and the doorways to the lesser rooms, where lay the ancient dead and our more recently perished. I disliked it down here and began to protest. "Madame, where…"

"There. My husband brought me down here when first we wed; he took me everywhere about the castle, insisting it was mine as much as his. As I say, I had forgotten."

"A door." I stared at the end of the passage, in which was set—yes, a door. Perhaps four feet high, it bore a stout lock, and its finish bloomed with damp. "Where does it lead?"

The Dowager moved closer to me. "That's just it. I'm not sure. Octavius told me when his ancestors built this castle they equipped it with a tunnel—an escape route. But I don't know where it goes. It may stretch to safety. It may open in the midst of Ortis's troops. It may have collapsed long ago." She looked at me with those pale green eyes. "It is like everything else in life, a coin with two sides. Good or ill."

"Madame, you must tell Rupert. It will have to be his decision whether to open that."

"You think so?"

"I do."

"But then I may be condemning him to death. If he goes through and I lose him also…" She began to weep like a woman brokenhearted. I took her in my arms, but soon enough she pulled herself together and said, "You are wise, Cindra. I will be guided by your opinion."

"Do you want me to tell him?" Take the burden from her shoulders.

And place it squarely on mine.

"I am so afraid. I am afraid we will die if we stay here. Afraid we will die or be captured if we venture out."

"My Queen, this route could be used by our soldiers to take Ortis by surprise. Or to send for help."

"If it has not collapsed. It is very, very ancient. Or if it does not collapse while our men are in it."

"Yes." A terrible risk.

She continued making her own argument. "Already, food grows scarce, and we still have weeks and weeks of winter ahead."

"I think we need to let Rupert decide. He is King. We cannot keep this information from him."

"As you say," she whispered, and turned and walked back the way we had come.

****

"I had no idea this was here," Rupert said later when I showed him the door to the tunnel. "Father never told me. I wonder why?"

I shrugged. Wrapped in a blanket against the pervasive chill, I thought about how much I detested this place where damp trickled across the floor and the walls bore patches of frost.

"Perhaps it has collapsed by now. But—"

"It may represent a chance for us. I have been thinking. If there were a way to reach our allies—or potential allies—in the West…I know of a few who might be willing to take on Ortis. King Edmund might, if only to keep us as a buffer."

"Do you think so?"

Standing there in the low light of a single torch, Rupert contemplated it, his damaged face full of doubt. "I don't know."

"What will you do, Husband?"

"Open up that door. See in what condition the escape tunnel lies. See, too, if we can determine in what direction it leads."

I laid my hand on his arm. "One bit of advice, if I may."

"I always welcome your advice, my love."

"Tell only a few. If it becomes widely known this is here, we may have a stampede of people demanding to be let through."

"Ah—very wise."

It would be a hard secret, though, to keep.

****

The door, when they attempted to open it, crumbled beneath their hands. The victim of damp, it revealed a dark, rough-worked hole that seemed to lead only into deeper darkness.

I did not attend the opening, of course. Rupert, who was there in the company of three carefully chosen men, told me about it later in the solitude of our chamber, one of the rare times we found ourselves alone.

I'd insisted he rest. We'd yet to spend a whole night together since his return, but now he lay on the bed, staring up at the canopy. The wind howled around the stones of the castle, and for the moment at least, the dreadful bombardment had ceased.

I came and climbed into the bed beside him. "What

did you see?" I urged.

"Only that—darkness."

"But it's not collapsed?"

"Not so far as we could tell."

"You did not venture in?"

He turned his head and looked at me. He studied me soberly before he said, "If it is to benefit us at all, it must travel a long distance beneath the ground. It is very old, no doubt as old as the castle, and barely shoulder high. Disturbing it after so long could cause a cave-in at any time, and that would prove certain death to anyone caught within."

"Oh."

"Cindra, I cannot in good conscience ask any man to take that risk."

For an instant I did not realize what he meant. I thought he refused out of hand to countenance use of the tunnel. Then I remembered the things I'd heard of him since his return, what his fellow soldiers said. In battle, he assigned no risk, no venture he would not first undertake himself.

"No," I breathed. "You cannot. You are King."

"Wife, I cannot…"

For once I interrupted him. "True, you cannot! You are needed here. Your people need you. I need you. Robin and your child—"

"I know, I know." He reached for me. "Please do not weep."

I hadn't realized that I did weep. "I am sorry I told you about it now! It is why your mother would not. She knows you better than I."

"No one knows me better than you." He kissed me, and the strength of it went through me, the claiming and belonging—but not enough to soothe my pain, not this time. "Cindra, love, no matter where I am or—or will be—I'm with you. So it was during the battles. So it will always be."

I began to sob in earnest. "Do not leave me. Do not leave me again. I could not bear it."

"Cindra, Wife, my strong one—look at me." He engaged my eyes. "Do you know what will happen if Ortis takes this castle? Death, destruction, and for many, slavery."

"I know, I know. But we are not yet beaten."

"Not yet, no. Ortis, deserted by his mercenaries, may yet give up the siege and go home to wait for better weather. But if not…" He gazed directly into my eyes. "If not, we will then be separated anyway. I will be executed. I shouldn't like to think what will happen to you, my wife and Queen, or to our child."

I folded my arms over that child protectively. I loved it fiercely, already, unseen.

Rupert rubbed a tear from my cheek. "Let us not get too far ahead of ourselves. Tomorrow I and my helpers will venture a short distance into the tunnel. It may be collapsed beyond where we can see." He smiled ruefully. "But I don't think so."

"What makes you say that?"

"We felt a draft coming down along it as soon as the door fell away. Cold it was, and the breath of it very bad. But a current of air."

"I want to be there when you go in."

"Out of the question."

"No, Rupert, I will be with you. To see you venture in—and come out again. Do not ask me to go about my business as if nothing is happening, not knowing…"

"As I say, tomorrow we will venture in only a few steps."

"Then there should be no risk to me, no reason I cannot be there."

He gazed at me long. "Very well. But under no circumstances are you to set foot inside, hear me? It is far too dangerous."

Not what I needed to hear.

But I said, "Understood. And now, come lie in my arms for a few minutes." Those few minutes were all we had.

Chapter Twenty-Two

The small team of three men chosen by Rupert had boarded up the opening after the door broke into rotting pieces. Early the next morning, I stood with my arms folded tight while they pulled the slats back off and I got my first glimpse of what lay beyond.

Two of the helpers were elderly, one quite young. The youngster fell back when the first breath issued from the tunnel, revealing his uneasiness.

I could not blame him. The air that came out felt deadly with chill and smelled like the grave—dark, stale, and poisonous.

It did not look like a tunnel so much as a hole dug into the dirt, its sides, floor, and roof—what little I could see—all curved.

We stood staring unhappily for a long moment before Rupert told Karl, one of the oldest helpers, “Hand me the light.”

“No.” The word came from my throat without my permission. I’d promised myself I would not interfere.

All three helpers looked at me sympathetically. Rupert did not spare me so much as a glance.

He took the torch from Karl’s hand, squared his shoulders, and ducked into the hole.

I started forward, unable to prevent that either. The other elder, Murgo, caught me back with a respectful, “Majesty, please—he said no.”

They had their instructions.

I stood there with that foul air hitting me in the face while my reason for living disappeared from sight.

He'd promised me he'd venture only a few steps. It seemed much farther. I saw the light fade and listened to the scrabbling sound of Rupert's progress.

Then—nothing!

I tore from Murgo's grasp. "Rupert!" I called.

"Hush, Majesty," Karl begged me. "You'll bring the roof down."

I bit my tongue. I held my breath.

The glow of Rupert's torch died to a faint thread before it began to increase again. Then we heard him moving closer, and I breathed once more.

He emerged wearing a grim expression and with dirt on his shoulders and shaved head. This he shook off before he turned to us.

"It extends some distance," he said.

Karl asked, "Could you tell, sire, in what direction?"

"Straight out, so far as I could see. South. We will need to calculate a trajectory."

"But it's not collapsed?" asked Murgo.

"Not that I could tell. The light did not travel far." His eyes moved to me and away again. "But the tunnel is very old and ready to come down—I feared the mere scuffing of my feet would bring it onto my head. I say we explore a bit farther, try to calculate the direction of the escape route, and resolve to use it only in the case of most extreme emergency. Meanwhile…" He eyed the three helpers severely before continuing, "not a word to anyone. I mean to clue Rellison in, but no one beyond the five of us is to know. Understand?"

They nodded gravely. I tried to be content. Only in the event of most extreme emergency, he said.

But did we not exist in the midst of that?

****

Crisis followed crisis, all calculated, so I felt, to drive me mad. During breaks in the weather—whenever the harsh wind stopped blowing—our attackers resumed their bombardment of our walls. Damage became critical, and supplies with which to repair any breech became scarce. Several interior walls were taken down for their stone. Even the boulders fired at us we utilized. I feared it would not be enough.

Truth be told, everything became scarce. Food most of all, followed by fuel for the fires. Quite apart from keeping our people warm, we needed fire for boiling the vats of water we dumped on the heads of any attackers bold enough to use a siege ladder.

Amidst all this, misery became endemic, as did things like lice. I am certain that helped to spread the new fever when it came.

Yet it started so slowly, with the children—a sick tot here, another there. Most of them had runny noses; their mothers didn't notice much else at first. Packed together so tightly in the ballroom, they shared food, bedding, and everything else. When the fever took them, they went one after the other, swiftly.

Rupert was with Rellison and others of his advisors, on a clear, frigidly cold day, when I realized the truth. I brought it to him in his council chamber, where he stood engaged in what appeared to be a grim conversation.

The others all rose to their feet when I came in, the old men like scarecrows wrapped in layers of clothing.

A few whispered, "Majesty."

I looked at my husband and for the first time in days, perhaps in weeks, truly saw him.

He appeared ill and aged from what he had been, his head freshly shaved. New lines scored his cheeks, and the wound near his eye had healed but badly, leaving a deep scar. I knew he bore other stubborn wounds beneath the clothing he wore, far too shabby for a king. Yet my heart nearly burst with love for him and ached for the news I brought.

His green eyes studied me before he asked in concern, "What is it? What's happened?"

I touched his arm and drew him away a step or two.

"I bring ill news."

His gaze dropped to the bulk of our child, now well grown and, at the moment, kicking. "Are you all right?"

"Yes."

"Wee Robin?"

"Fine." So far.

"Then, what?"

"I've just come from the ballroom." Where most of the women and children lived. "Rupert, the children are falling ill."

"Little ones always fall ill in winter. And crammed so close together…"

"This is not a simple ague. Fever, Rupert. At least ten of them, and still more with symptoms." Far more.

"No." He breathed the word, and in his eyes I saw his desire to deny it, the same I'd felt for days.

With regret I said, "I fear so. I did not want to bring word to you until I felt certain."

"Majesty?" asked Rellison, frowning and taking a

step toward us.

Rupert held up a hand to him, staring at me. “And you went there?”

“Of course I went there. I go every day to speak with the women, most of them widows, and to help with lessons. What I fear is they will all fall ill, the mothers of the sick first and then the rest of them. They share blankets, beds, food, and the privies.”

“I do not want you to go there again.”

The comment, so out of character, made me stare at him. “What?”

“I will not have you risk yourself and our child. Do you hear?”

Rupert had never before raised his voice to me. He did so now, turning every head in the room. I’d been bellowed at before, of course—by Cook in the kitchen and by Mother all my life. But this order came backed by the love I saw in Rupert’s eyes, so strong it might blind me, and the fear behind it.

“My darling,” I said softly, “I must. They are our people—my people. And they need me.”

“No.” Rupert, never stubborn, refused to back down now. Instead, with all his advisors watching, he pulled me into his arms. “I want you to go to the tower room. Stay there. Do not come out until we determine the nature of this sickness.”

“Sickness, sire?” Rellison picked up the word.

We had no choice but to tell them all, then. Many of them had family, widowed daughters or daughters by marriage, and grandchildren among those in the ballroom. The news was not taken well.

Rellison immediately told me, “Majesty, I can but agree with the King. You should separate yourself from the epicenter as completely as possible. Do you still feel well?"

I considered the question. I felt exhausted, constantly hungry, and quite heavily pregnant. I never felt truly well.

But I replied, "I have no symptoms."

"Not yet, perhaps." Rupert's hands tightened on my shoulders. I met his gaze and saw the truth: someone cared for me—me, Cinder-Ugly—and I was worth much to this man. He, with his humble bearing, great heart, and boundless courage, loved me.

And yes, I might matter to our people—at that moment I knew I mattered most to him.

"Perhaps, Majesty," Rellison suggested gently, "you might consent to retire to the tower just until we determine the extent of the contagion."

Answering not him but the love in Rupert's eyes, I replied, "I could do that, yes."

Relief flooded Rupert. "Rellison, please have all available physicians sent to the children's room. And, all of you, please pray for those innocents."

Chapter Twenty-Three

"What have you done with your shoes?"

Rupert, lying atop our bed like a man half-slain, squinted at my feet where I lay beside him. I knew we had only moments before he was called away again. I also knew he needed the reassurance of my company and my voice in his ears.

I answered simply, "Oh, I gave them to Markka. She had none."

He shot me an incredulous look. "She had no shoes?"

"Well, she did. But they were all broken and falling off her feet. It is cold where she is, and as I am confined here, I thought she should have my stout ones."

I could see Rupert did not like that. He propped himself up on one elbow. "And where did you get those? They look like the cat dragged them in after a hard night in the wet."

I laughed softly and wiggled my feet atop the coverlet. "These? They were mine when I slaved in Mother's kitchen among the hearth ashes. Cinder-Ugly, remember?"

"Yes, I remember." He did not like that, either. "We must be able to find you something better."

"Like your boots, which have been halfway through the wars and back again? We all go without, my love."

"I know we all go without; I do not mind depriving myself. But seeing you go without—it pierces my heart. My love, you were deprived long enough."

I gazed into his eyes. "That merely taught me not to mind. I have you and our child—I have more than I ever dreamed."

He caressed my cheek. "Only you could say such a thing." He kissed me, and for a moment I forgot everything else, the worry, the fear and exhaustion. Our hearts beat together until our child kicked hard.

We both laughed.

Rupert said then, "I will find you something better than those poor slippers—so I do vow."

"Just be sure and look after yourself," I told him, "when you are parted from me."

****

The weather raged, as did the fever in the castle below me. When the clouds broke—seldom enough—I used the perspective from my windows as a lookout, disheartened to learn Ortis's troops had shrunk no farther. I sent messages via Gerta to Rellison and the other advisors, Rupert being usually on the walls with the defenders. Oh, how I feared for him!

I feared for us all.

The first deaths from fever came quickly. Three little ones it was, then a slew of them, followed by several of their mothers.

I asked to go to them, longed to assure myself Markka, her daughter Dinnie, and wee Robin were still well. I might just have defied Rupert and gone to them, had someone not visited me first.

She came in mid-afternoon when the bombardment had once more commenced. I'd just begun wondering where Ortis continued to come by his ammunition. My intermittent views told me he'd cut down many of our fine trees and hurled them at us in pieces, which we then used for fuel after repairing the damage they caused. Some of the stones they catapulted, as I say, we also used to make repairs; others we tumbled back down on Ortis's troops. Several, I suspected, must have been fired back and forth many times.

When a fist pounded on my door, I thought it might be news about the progress of the contagion. I hauled it open immediately.

Mother stood there, head held at a haughty angle, swathed like everyone else in a blanket against the cold. Most folks wore their own bedding.

I moved instinctively to bar her from entering the room, but she pushed her way in, actually brushing my arm, from which she then recoiled fastidiously.

"You'll not keep me out," she said.

I stood and contemplated my options. I could use this as an excuse to leave the tower, shut her in, and go below. I could find Rupert and complain of her. I could stay and listen to yet another of her harangues filled with demand. I could think of no other reason she'd come to me.

Despite her haughtiness, she looked unwell, pale and sickly with something still very much wrong with her face, which had once contained so much beauty. Now it seemed to have sagged like putty, come a little bit apart at the seams as if the surgery she'd endured had not held.

Perhaps, then, pity made me come back into the room and close the door behind me.

"Madame Bulgar, what do you want?"

" 'Madame Bulgar,' " she mocked, her lips pursing in a cruel parody of mine. "You truly should call me Mother."

"I will not. I think you should go."

Instead she glanced around the room. "No fire? I thought you'd be all warm and cozy here."

"There's not enough fuel, Madame."

"At least you can't hear the bombardment so loudly here." Her ruined face twisted. "The constant banging, banging is driving me mad. All of it's driving me mad. You have to do something."

I drew my blanket closer around my shoulders. "What can I do? I told you before, we all must share in this misery; we all must endure."

She turned burning eyes on me; at that moment she did indeed appear mad. "You know, you look little different than you did back in my house, standing there in your ragged coverings. Even your slippers are the same. I asked you before and you would not say: how did you do it? How did you entrap him when my beautiful daughters could not?"

"Your beautiful daughters, Madame, are selfish and mean, with small, petty spirits that make them ugly." I used the word deliberately. This confrontation had been some twenty years in the making. And—so I thought—I had little left to lose. "They have, in fact, taken after you."

It cost me to say that. I still feared her, deep down inside—still shrank from her cruelty and hate. Yet Rupert's love wrapped around me like the blanket on my shoulders. She was, I told myself, nothing but a nasty, broken woman.

I thought the denouncement would send her into

one of her rages. Instead she smiled at me. "You think yourself so high and mighty. We are still your family—all you have left."

"You're wrong: I have Robin—the grandson you rejected."

"He will surely die, locked in that ballroom, the very heart of the fever. Cindra, you owe us. Get us out of that cesspool down there. I bid you again, bring us up here to live with you before we all fall ill."

For an instant I considered it—contemplated trading places with them, giving them this aerie. I even, heaven help me, thought about imprisoning them here, boarding up the door and leaving them with one another. Given all the noise below, no one would hear their screams.

But this place, these few square feet of space, represented our garden, my and Rupert's only opportunity to snatch a moment of rest and rejuvenation here and there. I knew he needed that even more than I did.

So I shook my head. "Go back to your assigned place and be grateful for it."

"Bitch." She narrowed her eyes. For an instant I felt sure she would attack me—I should have taken warning. "You selfish, selfish wretch. I fed you; I housed you all those years. Is this how you repay me?"

"Yes." Food had been all she offered me, and others' leavings, at that.

"At least think of your sisters, if you detest me so much."

"My sisters? And all the loving kindness they showed me?"

"So this is your revenge? Ugly does as ugly is."

"You should know, Madame. It seems I learned from the best." I stepped to the door and hauled it open. "Now please leave."

She eyed me speculatively. "When are you due?"

"Any day."

"Aren't you afraid it will be born like Robin's child? Like you?"

I shook my head. "Please go."

She took a step to pass me, and I felt a rush of relief; it was over. She would go—as a thousand times before, I could set about repairing myself.

In a low, vicious voice she said, "You won't know what it's like till something so ugly issues from your womb. Better it's born dead."

I stiffened. "Leave. If you won't, I will." I'd go straight to Rupert, have him imprison her. The woman represented a danger.

Her gaze narrowed with spite. "Go ahead."

I took one step, two before I felt her palms at my back. The tower stairs lay right outside the door—narrow and treacherous—and she shoved me straight down them with no time to catch myself or break the fall.

I remember catapulting down the flight like a pea down a chute, panic seizing my mind. And following that came only darkness.

Chapter Twenty-Four

"Cindra, Cindra!" A voice called my name, snared my consciousness, and drew me out of the darkness.

Rupert's voice.

Memory returned to me in pieces. The darkness first, the steepness and violence of the descent down the staircase, the cruelty in my mother's eyes.

My child.

I moaned and folded my arms across my belly. Every separate part of me hurt. I could not assess the damage, but I did know I could no longer feel the child.

I screamed.

Rupert picked me up from the pallet where I lay and into his arms. "All right, love. It's all right."

"Best not to move her, Your Highness," said another voice. "Her head…"

Rupert, bless him, did not release me. For several precious moments he held me to him and I felt the pounding of his heart.

Then he breathed, "Yes, your head." He laid me back down with infinite care.

I searched his face—pale, pinched, worn. "Our child?"

A smile broke across his countenance like sunshine. "Fine, he is fine. Born—"

"A son?"

"A fine son. Healthy, perfect."

"I don't remember."

The physician stepped forward. "Forgive me, Majesty, you were unconscious. We delivered the child, as we were not at all certain you would live."

"A boy."

"A Prince," the physician corrected softly.

Rupert said, "I thought I was going to lose you." He lowered his forehead to my hands. "I could not bear it."

"She pushed me. My mother—"

"What?" He raised a face transformed by rage. "What!"

"You did not know? She came to the tower. When I refused to do as she asked, she shoved me down the stairs." And then she must have gone, left me lying there. Her daughter and her grandchild. She stepped over me and told no one.

"She did not bring help?" I asked.

Rupert shook his head. "I came up to see you. I had a feeling…I found you lying in a heap where the stairs make that tight turn. If not for that, you would have tumbled all the way down."

I shuddered. "What have I broken?"

Rupert and the physician exchanged glances. But Rupert said, "Nothing save your head. There are scrapes and bruises aplenty."

"Your waters broke, Majesty, in the fall," the physician told me.

"I must go and deal with your mother," Rupert said. "See to it she is arrested and punished."

"No."

"No?"

"Not before I see our son and hold him. Where is

he? I want him in my arms."

They both helped me to sit up, my head going around in slow circles. The physician in attendance summoned another, who came with a small bundle in his arms.

Tiny—he was so tiny when I held him, so small to make up a large part of my world. He had but a fuzz of fair hair and grave, dark eyes.

"You are certain he's all right?"

Rupert smiled. "He came into the world hollering, and look—he's perfectly made." Rupert gently unfolded the swaddling to reveal our son's limbs. I wrapped him again and cuddled him to my breast.

The physicians having melted away, we sat so for an instant—two become three. And nothing else mattered, not the continuing bombardment nor the fact we were trapped like rats in a hole. My life became beautiful and complete.

Then Rupert said softly, "You realize she will have to pay for this. I do not understand, Cindra—she must have known you would be able to tell what she'd done to you."

Our eyes met. Reluctantly, I admitted, "I do not suppose she expected me to survive the fall. I saw the expression on her face, Rupert, just before she shoved me—one of pure hate."

"Did she care nothing for the welfare of her grandchild?"

"I believe she cares for no one but herself. She uses others to get what she wants. She came saying my sisters needed refuge from the fever, but there's no real concern for them behind it."

Rupert drew himself up. Ragged, worn, and bone-thin, at that instant he nevertheless looked every inch the King.

"She will pay this time for the crime she has committed—treason—and all the other times she's hurt you. I will see her hang. From the battlements."

I closed my eyes on a wave of pain. "Rupert—"

"No, love. I would acquiesce to you in almost anything. Not this."

****

The north wall fell the next day while Rupert pronounced sentencing on my mother in the confines of the council chamber, there being nowhere else to stage a hearing. She'd been taken into custody the night before and held in the depths of the castle all night. Rupert told me, as I did not attend, that she screamed threats and hollered abuse the whole time, claiming my accusation against her was a lie—she had never been to our chamber in the tower, never spoken with me, let alone pushed me.

"My daughter the Queen wishes to destroy me! She is envious and has always hated me."

Rupert, so he told me, informed her she had committed high treason against me and the Crown Prince. He passed sentence of hanging, and our world came apart.

Yes, to be sure it had been crumbling by pieces all the winter long, since last fall, truly, when war broke out. But now it happened quite literally, a well-placed series of missiles collapsing the whole stone face on one side, leaving us as good as defenseless.

Though I had not attended Mother's trial, I insisted I should be at her sentencing even though Rupert objected. I felt I needed to face her, especially given her claims made during her arrest. So sore I could barely stand, and limping badly, I left my new child in the midwife's care and entered the council chamber, the jailer and all Rupert's advisors, including Rellison, standing by.

Mother looked like a madwoman, an animal. Fresh from the depths of the castle, she wore only the garments in which she'd been clothed at the time of her arrest, now rent and marked by patches of damp.

Her face frightened me. Often in the past that had been so. In truth, I'd feared her all my life but never so much as now. Eyes stretched wide and mouth open in a rictus, she was barely recognizable.

She focused on me only briefly before looking away again, completely absorbed in herself. Except for one flash of hate, I am not sure she actually acknowledged my presence, the only of her daughters to attend her in her extremity. For neither Bethessa nor Nelissa showed. Perhaps fear kept them away. Certainly, respect did not bring them.

Nor did love. I stood there listening to Rupert pronounce death on this woman who had been so hateful to me and realized she went to her death with no one—absolutely no one—caring for her.

At that moment, the wall fell.

The bombardment, to be sure, continued most of the time. We had become very nearly inured to it. Now the end of the world came with a great, sliding rumble like the worst thunder ever heard, shaking the castle to its foundations.

A moment of intense silence followed. Rupert, who had just spoken the sentence of death by hanging to Mother, stopped speaking. Everyone else in the chamber froze. Rupert and Rellison stared at one another.

Then we heard screams, cries of alarm, and a great roar from the throats of Ortis's army outside. My heart fell so violently I swayed.

"What was that?" Incredibly, Mother broke the silence. "What's happened?"

Rupert whispered, "The walls."

Everyone vacated the chamber—which had no windows—and ran to see. Even the jailer left Mother unattended; she must have run at that moment.

I followed Rupert, limping painfully, to the nearest exterior windows, which happened to be in a sitting room. Windows there were already thronged, but folk made way for the King, his advisors, and me.

I looked out and saw…

But I have no words even now to describe it.

Have I mentioned that the castle had once been a beautiful structure? Built of pale amber stone, it had graceful, curved battlements and curtain walls, one of which now lay crumbled like the blocks of a child's toy.

Dust and debris still floated in the clear morning air—no weather to defend us now. And already I saw Ortis's soldiers scrambling over the wreckage like ants over a pile of sugar cubes, seeking entry.

"God help us all," Rellison breathed.

I glanced into my husband's face, less my husband at that moment than the King. I thought I saw our very defeat reflected in his eyes.

"What happens now?" I whispered.

His face twisted. "Now we fight. Hand to hand, if need be—with whatever weapons we can raise."

I thought of all the women in the castle, all the children and aged. The sick. How could they fight? All those people—my people—had just been doomed.

Rupert must have reached the same conclusion, or maybe he'd always held this eventuality in the back of his mind. He turned to me and seized me by the shoulders.

"Go get Robin and Octavius."

Octavius. We'd decided to name our son after Rupert's father.

"Yes."

"Quick as you can, love. Go through the tunnel."

"What?"

"Swiftly, now. Wrap up warm."

I stared into my husband's face, uncomprehending. "But we have not explored the tunnel. We do not know…"

"Still." Agony flooded his eyes. "It is your best chance. Go to King Edmund if you can. Tell him you bring the heir to my kingdom."

"But what of you? What of everyone here?"

"Do this." He captured both my hands and carried them to his lips. "Do it for me."

I knew it then: he meant to stay, to fight and die here. If I went through the tunnel, I would never see him again.

He could tell the moment I comprehended the truth—he must have seen horror fill my eyes.

"My love goes with you," he vowed, "and I will love you forever."

"Promise you will follow if you can," I begged.

"I do so promise." But I knew he harbored no such expectation. Not the man to flee, he would perish with the majority of his people.

I caught my breath, turned, and ran.

Chapter Twenty-Five

I collected Markka along with Robin, Octavius, and Markka's wee daughter, Dinnie, refusing to tell her where we were bound. I then spent precious moments attempting to persuade the Dowager Queen to accompany us.

The castle now lay in a state of mad fear, panic, and confusion. Hand-to-hand fighting had already broken out on the north side of the building. I knew Rupert would be bound for there—would likely die there also. I tried to close my mind to that and, with Octavius in my arms, towed my charges to the lower levels.

Where the Dowager stuck. She refused to leave the King's tomb and, throwing herself across it, declared she did not care where we were bound or if the castle fell around her.

"I wish only to be with him."

I kissed her cheek and left her—the closest to a loving mother I had ever known.

"Where are we bound?" Markka asked breathlessly as we continued on.

I paused long enough to shoot her an assessing look. "I suppose I should give you a choice."

"Choice?" she gasped.

"The castle is going to fall. We face capture and death. But there may be a way out."

"How?"

"A tunnel. Very old and dangerous. It hasn't been explored and may not still be intact."

"You mean…"

"It might well collapse on us." Which might just be a kinder death than what Ortis had in store. "However, Rupert thinks it's the best chance for getting the children out—the heir to the throne."

"Oh."

"It's up to you, Markka. You can come with us or you can turn back. I beg you only to speak not of our escape."

Eyes wide and hair streaming, she stared. "Where is this tunnel?"

"I will show you."

In truth, the black hole stretching into what seemed like infinity looked even more terrifying than I remembered. When I pulled the boards away, Markka shied.

"That? Majesty, I don't know that I can. I—I am afraid of the dark."

"We will take a torch and be able to use it most of the way, till we near the end." Heaven help me, I did not want to enter that bolt-hole alone. Or at all.

"But it is so narrow, and we have the children. How far does it stretch?"

"I do not know." The longer we stood debating it, the worse the prospect seemed. Foul air issued from the tunnel like breath from a decayed mouth.

Yet I could hear the sounds of fighting going on far above us, and I remembered the look in Rupert's eyes.

Markka bit her lip, juggling the child on her hip, and considered me. "I cannot send you alone, Majesty, and you just having given birth. But I'm afraid."

"As am I, Markka. Here, if you can carry Dinnie and Robin, I will go first with Octavius and the light. Just pull those boards across behind us so no one can tell where we've gone."

How to describe that journey? I'd faced many a terrible thing during my lifetime. None required as much courage as crawling into that hole. And when Markka obediently drew the boards up after us, shutting us in with the damp, foul air, I wanted nothing so much as to flee.

But no, I must have wanted one thing more after all—to preserve the life of Rupert's child, now only one day old. For I pressed on, and Markka behind me, she sobbing quietly all the while.

I counted the steps under my breath: a score, two score, a hundred. The tunnel lay ahead of us like the trail of a snake, only the shortest portion of which the torch revealed to us. We went bent double, the children and the torch clutched in our hands, and the ceiling fell down on us, pattering gently onto our heads and backs like rain. The curved sides crumbled; clods broke loose and slithered to our feet.

And most terrifying of all, the torch flickered. The rational portion of my mind knew it for a good thing. It meant air moved along the passage, which must mean, in turn, the tunnel had not collapsed up ahead.

I feared all the while for the children breathing that air, especially Octavius, new born. What if I killed him in my attempt to save him? A hundred times I peered into his little face, tucked against me, to make sure he breathed.

Dinnie, perhaps in response to her mother's sobs,

began to wail also. The sound lifted the hairs on my neck.

"What if the light goes out?"

The same question had been in my own mind. I told Markka, trying desperately to sound calm, "Then we feel our way—either backward or forward."

She whispered in fervent response, "Please God, do not let the light go out."

Time elongated impossibly, as did distance. I could not tell how long we had been half crawling along, nor how far we'd gone. I could not even estimate in which direction the tunnel extended or where we might emerge—another frightening prospect.

We came upon the first partial collapse unexpectedly. The light showed it to me too late, and I almost ran into the waist-high pile of dirt before I stuttered to a stop. Above, part of the ceiling had come down—how much I could not at once tell.

Behind me Markka whimpered, "What—?"

"A collapse."

"No, God, no! What will we do?"

"Hush. Let me see how bad it is. Can you take Octavius?"

She whimpered again. Her arms already full of unhappy children, she accepted my infant.

I stuck the end of the torch into the soft dirt and, hoping I didn't trigger further collapse, thrust my arms into the ancient soil that lay ahead of me. Cold as the grave it felt and clammy with damp. Yet I wanted so desperately to move forward.

Behind lay only capture and death.

Ahead lay the unknown.

"Majesty, can you get through?"

"I think so." I dug like a badger through the soft soil—the only saving grace being that it was not hard-packed. I scrabbled and fought and dragged myself through to a clear space before I reached back for the torch, very nearly setting my arm on fire.

"Pass me the children, carefully."

Markka did, her face a mask of fear, and crawled through after.

"Here." I handed back Dinnie, who fretted for her mother, and Robin. "The way ahead looks clear."

"How much farther?"

"I do not know, but it looks as if it begins to slope upward."

"A good sign?"

"It can only be."

****

We climbed and crawled and hauled ourselves through two more semi-collapses, only to be brought up short when the tunnel branched.

Branched!

Nothing had prepared me for this. It now seemed we'd been down here forever and might continue so. I'd concentrated on putting one foot—or knee—in front of the other, thinking the tunnel our one escape route. Now I must make a choice.

When I stopped abruptly, poor Markka, who could see little but my back, asked, "What now? Another fall?"

"No." I squeezed to one side and showed her the impossible—not one black hole ahead but two leading away at angles.

"What does it mean?"

"The tunnel branches."

"Which way—?"

"I don't know." My overwrought brain sought desperately for an answer. I tried to picture the castle and the lay of the tunnel leading from it—southward, which was good. Surely we'd come far enough to lead us away from the walls and would be safe whichever path we took?

Of one thing I felt certain: we could not stay where we were.

Both openings seemed narrower than what we'd been traversing, dismayingly so. Air still moved down both of them but seemed a little stronger as it issued from the branch on the right, which I figured must veer west.

Faced with the impossible, I caught my breath and chose. "This way. Here, you go first with Dinnie and Robin. I will hold the light."

Was it instinct that made me change the order of things? I'll never know. But Markka entered the tunnel on the right obediently. It collapsed just after I followed her, dirt raining around me—and Octavius pressed against me—in a clammy shower, clods both great and small trapping my legs and threatening to choke me.

I heard Dinnie wail. Markka exclaimed in horror, and the torch went out.

Chapter Twenty-Six

A grave—I was caught in a grave, or half caught in one. The darkness of the grave could not be more complete than what surrounded us. I could still hear Markka sobbing as the last of the dirt settled. And—praise be to God—I could feel Octavius moving in my arms. I'd been buried to my knees. I reached for Markka, blind in the darkness.

"Pull me out!"

"The torch!"

"I know. For the love of God, pull me—"

Hampered by both children, she tried. In the end, I again passed Octavius into the crook of her arm and fought my own way free, kicking and thrashing and very likely risking a further downfall. I didn't care by then—I was trapped in darkness.

Once free, I collapsed, but not for long. I fought my way to my feet and accepted my son back from Markka.

"What now?" she wept. "What…"

"Feel our way. I'll go first."

"Can't. No room for you to get by. We're stuck like corks in a bottle. Oh, I can't breathe!"

"There's still air. I can feel it moving. Are the children all right?"

"Yes. Yes." They both wailed.

"Then we go on—you first. Feel your way along

the wall."

"I can't, Majesty!"

"You have to, for the sake of the children."

We went, step by painful step, Markka groping with one hand along the wall while I carried both Robin and Octavius. She sobbed all the while and whispered over and over again, "I can't."

Behind us—and ahead—the darkness stretched. I could not tell where we went, save upward, slowly. I could think only of getting out from under the ground, that and of the weight of dirt pressing down upon us. If the tunnel collapsed now—fore or aft—we would never be found.

It did not collapse. Instead, at last I realized the air had begun to grow lighter around us. I could very faintly see the curve of the roof and Markka's bulk moving ahead of me.

"Majesty, I can see—"

"Yes! And there's air. Fresh air!" I could have wept. Markka did weep, and she sped her pace to a scrambling run.

Only to come up against a wall of dirt. The light shone down from above us, through roots and fallen soil. No way up.

"What—" Markka broke off.

We could hear through the opening, the sounds of distant shouts, cries—the clash of arms.

Distant.

Breath surged in my lungs. "I think we're safe away."

"Where?"

"I don't know."

"How are we to get up?"

I examined the shaft—barely wide enough for our shoulders, it stretched some ten feet upward. The fallen dirt clogged it part way. But I could feel the air—cold—and see the sky full of gray cloud. I could have wept for joy and frustration.

"We move this dirt and climb out," I told Markka.

"Climb?"

I turned and looked at her. "After what we've just accomplished, this is nothing." *Nothing*. I hurt from head to toe and—somewhere back in the fall—I'd lost one shoe. Yet freedom lay only ten feet above us.

Markka took heart from my determination. She nodded. "Yes, Majesty. You are right. Come, children, see that? It's the sky, freedom. And that's where we're bound."

****

We cleared what dirt we could from beneath the shaft, and carved steps into what was left with found stones. That being done, we dug toe holds into the shaft as far as we could reach. Higher up, roots stuck through the soil—hand holds, I hoped.

I took off my shawl and fashioned a carrier of it. Fortunately, none of the children had much bulk or weight. We looked at each other.

Markka, wild-eyed and wild-haired, her face streaked with dirt and tears, visibly drew herself up. "I will go first, Majesty. I am better fit—you gave birth but yesterday."

Giving me no opportunity to argue it, she put the sling around her neck with the makeshift cradle at the back. I placed Dinnie into it, knowing Markka needed both hands free. If she fell, she would crush her own child.

I wanted to close my eyes, shut away the sight of her making that perilous climb. Fear wouldn't let me. I watched her scramble, slither, slide, and at last haul herself up onto her belly at the top. She and her daughter were safe.

She turned to look at me.

Doubt hit me then. She might leave me. Even after all we'd been through together, that thought possessed my mind. My mother would have abandoned me. So would my sisters. Donella—the only other friend I'd known—might have stayed.

What of Markka?

She cast me a single look before turning her gaze away, glancing about.

"We're in the wood, well beyond the edge of town, Majesty. The castle is far away. It—it is burning!"

My heart clenched and fell. Rupert! I saw the terror in Markka's face, silhouetted against the gray sky. Now was the moment she would panic and run.

Instead she very gently lifted her daughter from the sling and tossed it down to me. "Put Robin in there—we will haul him up next. Then you and Octavius. Do you need me to come back down and help you?"

I just stood there, tears pouring down my face.

She never knew why.

****

I crawled my way up to find we had, indeed, emerged in a little copse of trees just outside the boundary of the town, a wild place no one had ever claimed, full of rocks and scrub bushes and ancient trees. Snow lay on the ground, and after our long, nearly airless time below, we shivered. I had only one shoe and that one woefully inadequate, being the aged slipper from my days in the kitchen. I didn't care, even though we had miles to walk before we might reach help.

We walked. Slowly and steadily, with the babes cradled in our arms, we moved through the gray day with the clamor of battle behind us.

I went for the sake of the children and not my own—for them and for Markka, who'd shown such courage and loyalty. My heart wanted to return to that place of conflict, to be with Rupert even if that meant dying with him.

As we went, it began to snow softly, big flakes floating down onto our hands and faces. We had to pause many times to nurse the children when they cried and, when I lost all feeling in my bare foot, to wrap it in pieces of the shawl.

That journey changed me, altered me fundamentally inside, and turned me into the woman I have since become. For all her painful experiences, Cinder-Ugly had been a child who still believed impossibly in a happily-ever-after. I now became Her Majesty Cindra the Queen, wife—or widow—of King Rupert, devoid of wealth but heavy with responsibility. I grew up. I grew grim. Having left my heart back with Rupert, I became a woman without one.

"What do you think is happening at the castle?" Markka asked this many times.

Having no answer for her, I shook my head.

Anything could be happening.

Ortis's forces might have overrun the place. The defenders might have repelled them, securing the broken wall. The fire might have consumed everything. They might all be dead.

Rupert might have lost his kingdom. He might have lost his life.

"Where will we go?"

"To Khett. King Edmund." Rupert's best ally, so he'd said.

Markka turned her head and stared at me. She no longer looked like Markka, who had been a rather pretty girl. She looked like a woman destroyed, her face a mask of dirt and pain. "So far?"

"So far."

"We'll never make it, Majesty. The children…"

"At least we can feed them."

"Yes, but we have no food. And you—"

I did not tell her I bled heavily; I could feel it. And the last of my strength had nearly failed.

She continued on a sob, "No food. No water. No rest."

We stumbled on, running on sheer willpower until night fell and a miracle occurred. We happened upon a woodsman's hut. There was no one inside—everyone had fled to the castle for protection.

Only look how that had served them!

We went in. I would not allow Markka to strike a light, but we did kindle a small fire in the hearth. There was food and a bed, and a chance to sleep.

Come morning, Markka wanted to stay there. I did not dare and told her if Ortis won the battle at the castle, his troops would spread out and occupy all the land.

"Yes, Majesty, but that will not happen for days. You need rest. You are not well."

"I need to get the Crown Prince to safety." Or he might be King by now. I could not, would not let myself think about that possibility.

"Just one day," Markka begged.

It terrified me; we were not far enough away. For the sake of the children and because it began to snow hard, I gave in.

The next morning, a second miracle occurred.

Chapter Twenty-Seven

Markka brought word when she returned from using the outhouse, her eyes shining.

"Majesty, Majesty, you'll never guess!"

I confess, a thousand thoughts burgeoned through my mind: Rupert had come looking for us; Ortis's army had fallen; We could go home. I shook my head.

"Horses. Two of them. In a shed out back. Do you think you can ride?"

I'd never been on the back of a horse. Scarcely had I ridden in a carriage. But the woman I'd now become had no room for uncertainty. "Yes."

We borrowed warm clothing, blankets, and food from our accidental host and set off riding through the newly fallen snow. The weather had cleared, but looking back toward the castle, I could no longer see so much as a wisp of smoke.

Setting our backs to home, we rode on.

The journey gave me an opportunity to think. Rupert knew King Edmund. I did not. Rupert might trust him; I no longer trusted anyone save Markka. If Ortis succeeded in overthrowing Burgendy, what was to stop him taking aim at Khett next?

"Markka," I said as we rode, "it would be best if we do not let anyone know who Octavius is, or that the Crown Prince of Burgendy has survived. That way, Ortis cannot hunt him down and kill him. That means we can tell no one who I am, either."

"But Majesty! How will you sue King Edmund for help if you do not tell him who you are?"

"I cannot, at least not at once. We must wait and see how the land lies. For now, I think we must pose as mere refugees. Sisters, perhaps." I smiled painfully. "Though I have never had a sister who cared for me."

"But Majesty…"

"To begin, you must stop calling me that."

"What shall I call you?"

"Cinders."

"But that is an insulting sort of name."

"And I am no one of consequence. We will say we were returning home when the castle fell and we came away. It will explain how we alone escaped. For I have seen no one else from the castle, have you?"

"Not yet," Markka admitted, and bit her lip. "We must say you were away at your lying in. It will explain why you have a newborn infant. Say you were unwed and in shame."

"A likely story."

She gave me an apologetic look. "It will mean you must remove your wedding band. I'm sorry; I know what it means to you."

A lump rose to my throat. I looked down at the fragile band, inscribed with flowers. Rupert had put it on my finger, and I'd never yet taken it off.

"I would do far more to protect my son. And it is but for a time, until we can discover how things lie in Khett and—and who is left alive back home."

"Yes." Markka gave me a tremulous smile. "Yes, Sister."

****

And so we arrived in the kingdom of Khett, two hapless and helpless peasant women with children. We played our parts well, if I do say it. And I'm certain we looked them also, dirty and ragged, the children weary and squalling and me with but one shoe.

The good citizens of Khett with whom we first came in contact passed us along like a hot potato; no one wished to keep us too long, until we came to King Edmund's palace.

Not exalted enough to see the King himself, we were at last conducted into the presence of an official, a middle-aged man with an impatient manner and not unkind eyes.

He introduced himself as Sir Rand and said, once he'd heard our story, "Quite frankly, we'd wondered what transpired in Burgendy. We have had absolutely no communication even via our agents."

"Agents?" I repeated in surprise.

"My good woman, we always have operatives in foreign capitals. It is as if ours have now dropped off the face of the earth. Not too surprising, given you say the castle has fallen."

"We thought we saw fire there," I replied carefully. "And the north wall had crumbled. We do not know if King Rupert and his family survived." I widened my eyes in what I hoped passed for innocence. "You do not know?"

Sir Rand shook his head. "Yours are the first words we have had of this." He rubbed his rather long chin. "I will have to inform the King. Meanwhile I suppose you request sanctuary?"

"Yes, sir, please," Markka said.

He eyed us unhappily. "Five dependents. The

kingdom of Khett, I will have you know, is not a charity. I hope you come prepared to work."

"As always," I agreed.

****

We never did achieve an audience with the King. I knew that had I spoken the truth of my identity, I'd have been conducted to him in a moment. But revealing my identity exposed Octavius to risk. So though I ached to throw myself on King Edmund's mercy and demand to know whatever he learned of the situation in Burgendy and most of all whether Rupert still lived as a prisoner or otherwise, I did not dare.

Markka and I, with the children, were given berths in a rooming house, a grim and lowly place run by an aging widow. She accepted us grudgingly and greeted us with the words, "I hope them children don't cry much. It'll disturb the clientele."

The clientele consisted of an unsavory and rather unfortunate sampling of Khett's poorest citizens. Markka and I found ourselves living in a garret, and when whatever stipend Sir Rand had given Mrs. Flick ran out, we worked to earn our beds.

I found myself back in the kitchen, working among the ashes once again.

Mrs. Flick needed the assistance. She ran the house by herself with the help of one idiot lad who barely understood what was said to him. At first Markka and I took turns minding the children, but even having been wed to a soldier, Markka's skills in the kitchen did not match my own.

My abilities at the hearth returned to me swiftly, as if they'd never left, which perhaps they hadn't. Heaven knew my stint as Queen had been short enough. Mrs.

Flick professed herself happy with the skills Cook had taught me and settled into calling me Miss Cinders.

We got what news we could from gossip, and that mostly overheard in the dining room. Mrs. Flick's guests, as I say, came and went. I took to leaving the door to the kitchen ajar, stretched my ears, and learned what I could.

Gossip being gossip, I did not know what to believe.

They said everyone in Burgendy was dead, from the rats in the cellars to the King, as they put it. Burned to death. Stabbed. Tortured. Heads cut off. Everyone had a different story. None of them lent me much hope. I cried a thousand tears into the ashes, salting Mrs. Flick's food with them. I raged and prayed and trembled, all with the blank face the landlady liked to see. My time of servitude in Mother's kitchen stood me in good stead.

At night, during my brief moments of rest, I cuddled Octavius in my arms and, sleepless, imagined a hundred scenarios. All returned always to one truth: they must be dead, every one. Else why would they not escape the castle, the city? Why not send for help?

My heart grieved for Rupert and the Dowager, for my close acquaintances—there were those for whom I cared, such as Rellison. I grieved for a life gone and the hope of regaining it.

If Burgendy had indeed fallen and Ortis lay in possession of the kingdom, what would he do? I pondered that long as well, because what he might do governed what I should. Had he any notion the Crown Prince—possibly King—of Burgendy survived? What might he do if he did? Hunt us down?

And if I went and threw myself on King Edmund's mercy, what would he do? Would he see this as an opportunity to take Ortis on and claim Burgendy for himself? Would he, too, want wee Octavius eliminated?

I might take that risk on my behalf—never on that of my son.

So the days crawled by, and winter—our old ally and defender—closed in for a vicious last showing. It snowed hard, the drifts filling the streets, and the wind howled like a mob of marauders. In fact sometimes I roused from my sleep with my heart pounding, thinking the north wall had fallen again.

I would lie there, remembering the expression in Rupert's green eyes the last time I saw him—fearful, protective, and so loving.

So we languished in obscurity, with no hope of forever.

Chapter Twenty-Eight

"Cinders, look lively! Stop with your moping and moaning, girl. Do you think I pay you to stand staring at the fire?"

Mrs. Flick did not, in fact, pay me. We worked for our keep and that of the children. But I nodded humbly.

"And make sure you keep those brats quiet until your sister gets back from market."

All three babes were, in fact, tucked into the corner, none of them fussing. But Mrs. Flick whacked me on the shoulder with a ladle in passing.

I sighed. At that moment it seemed my life had brought me in a circle. Save for Octavius's existence, the days spent with Rupert might have been nothing more than a fevered dream.

Markka returned soon enough, her cheeks flushed with cold and excitement. Without shedding her cloak, she edged up to me. "Sister, word is all over the market…"

"Neither do I pay you to gossip." Mrs. Flick struck Markka across the back of the head. "Give me the basket."

Markka handed it over, her excitement contagious. "But Mistress Flick, everyone in town is saying—word has come from Burgendy."

"No." I breathed it between parted lips as hope and dread drenched me by turns. "What word?"

Even Mrs. Flick stopped to listen.

But Markka shook her head. “No one seems to be sure. Just that a small delegation came to see King Edmund. They arrived on horseback, so swaddled against the cold no one could identify them.”

Rupert, I thought. And then: No, don’t be foolish, and don’t long for the impossible.

“It might be a delegation from King Ortis,” Mrs. Flick proposed. “Everyone in the former kingdom of Burgendy has been conquered.”

I knew that to be the accepted premise. But Markka wanted to argue it. “Still, Mistress Flick, should you hear anything…”

“Such as?”

“News of anyone looking for us—”

“That’s right, you had people there, didn’t you?” Mrs. Flick sniffed. “I dare say the likes of you two have no importance to anyone left alive.”

Or far too much importance for our safety.

****

I had no sleep that night, but next day life went on just as it had, me working among the cinders, Markka minding the children and lending a hand where she could. Since Mrs. Flick needed nothing from the market, she did not send Markka out, and no word came by other means. Mrs. Flick’s boarders brought no gossip—at least none that I heard through the kitchen door—and the spark of hope in my heart died to almost nothing.

Day after day dragged past so. I do not mind admitting I wept in my corner by the fire and repeated over and over again that if a party had indeed come from Burgendy, it must be Ortis’s men bent on negotiating with King Edmund.

My husband must be dead.

Then, on a bright, cold morning, Mrs. Flick sent Markka to the market once again. Before she left, Markka whispered to me, “I will not come back until I learn something.”

She did not return for several hours. Mrs. Flick complained, then raged and took her annoyance out on me, busy with both my kitchen chores and minding the children.

But when Markka at last arrived, she came with her face alight. Leaving the yard door open, she rushed straight to me, ignoring Mrs. Flick’s presence.

“Majesty—”

“What did you call her?” Mrs. Flick demanded sharply.

“Sister. There are men, two of them—”

“Shut that door! Do you think I want the world peering into my kitchen?”

Markka hastened to obey, but before she did I caught a hint of the soft air. Spring. Was our terrible winter at an end?

Markka grasped my hands and looked into my eyes. “Cindra, I have learned that only two men came from the kingdom of Burgendy, one older and one younger. Nobody seems to know just who they are, but they’ve been to see Kind Edmund, and they are said to be searching for a woman.”

I stared at her like the dense, stupid creature I’d become, nothing more than an obedient drudge. Even my hope refused to stir…much.

She jiggled my hands. “They have been everywhere, asking. They must come here, we must assure it…"

Mrs. Flick, her features heavy with a frown elbowed in. "Looking for a woman? What mad tale is this? What woman?"

Markka turned bright eyes on Mrs. Flick. "The Queen of Burgendy." Markka waved a hand. "She is here."

"What?" Mrs. Flick began to laugh, a harsh, rusty sound seldom heard. "Here, where?"

Markka touched my shoulder. "This is the Queen of Burgendy."

Mrs. Flick turned and surveyed me, head to foot. I knew how I must appear with my hair—never my best feature—straggling down my back, my worn dress covered with ashes, and my feet wrapped in rags.

"This?" Mrs. Flick repeated. "This ugly thing is the queen of nothing, save the cinders. Get to work and mind those brats unless you wish to feel the weight of my hand. And, girl, stop telling wild stories."

For once Markka refused to back down. "I tell no tales, Mistress Flick."

"Just gossip you've heard in the market."

"Yes! Should the men come here, you must let them see Cindra. You cannot keep her shut away in this kitchen."

"I will do nothing of the kind. She is a servant."

"She is wife to King Rupert, if he still lives."

"No one in Burgendy has survived, stupid girl, save possibly these two men of whom you speak."

"Nay, but listen, Mistress. It's said they look for a woman with a babe."

My knees threatened to give way beneath me; for the first time Mrs. Flick hesitated. Her gaze darted to the children.

Markka turned to me. “Tell her, Majesty, tell her.”

I parted my lips; words would not come. What if these were not Rupert’s but Ortis’s men after all, seeking to find and eliminate the Crown Prince? What if I endangered Octavius?

Mrs. Flick turned hard eyes on me. “She is too stupid to speak; she is surely too stupid to be a queen. And too ugly. Get to work, both of you.”

Markka made so bold as to touch Mrs. Flick on the arm. “But should these men come to your door, please—”

Mrs. Flick drew away, sneering. “And how shall I know them?”

“Folk in the market say one of them carries a shoe.”

“A shoe! Now I know you are mad.” Mrs. Flick clouted Markka in the side of the head.

Anger flared in Markka’s eyes. I could only wish for her courage, but that which I’d possessed as Rupert’s wife—which had got me through the terror of the tunnel—seemed to have deserted me. I had reverted to the cowed creature who’d lived beneath my mother’s heel.

We got to work, both of us, but I whispered to Markka as soon as I dared, “A shoe? Whatever can it mean?”

****

We found out soon enough. Markka snuck out early the next morning, slipping through the kitchen door, which was strictly forbidden unless Mrs. Flick sent one of us.

I arose as always, tucked the babes into their

corner, and got to work with a will, hoping to avert Mrs. Flick's anger. But when she came into the kitchen and did not see Markka, she demanded, "Where is your sister?"

I looked up at her and lied, "Not well. In the privy, I think."

"Wasting time, you mean. She's become a slacker. You will have to work twice as hard."

"Yes, Mrs. Flick."

"Our guests will want their breakfast soon. I expect the food on the table in ten minutes. And keep those children quiet."

"Yes, Mrs. Flick."

The woman left the kitchen, and Markka burst in. She seized hold of my shoulders with both hands. "Majesty, Majesty!"

"Don't call me that."

Her eyes blazed. "The story is true. I saw the two men, though only from a distance. Yet—" She broke off before resuming, "They go from house to house. I begged all who would listen to direct them here."

"What—?"

"I bid them know they might, beneath this roof, find what they sought."

I stared at her, aghast. "Markka! You may have just condemned Octavius to death."

"Or restored to him his rightful place. Majesty, dear friend…" Her eyes flooded with tears. "Since we've been here I have watched you change from a graceful, confident woman to…this! A drudge among the cinders. You must find your courage. You must take a chance."

"And if they are Ortis's men? If they snatch

Octavius from my arms?"

"Believe. Have faith. They will not."

I bent my head and wept.

Chapter Twenty-Nine

Those who tell the story have some parts of it right. Of course, it being a tale meant for entertainment, they seek to beautify everything.

They tell of a prince traveling from house to house carrying a crystal slipper. Can you imagine such a thing? What woman, however delicate, would dare to wear a shoe made of glass, for fear of breaking it and cutting her foot to shreds?

But yes, the men did come looking. And they came with a shoe.

I remained working hard among the cinders until I heard a commotion from the front part of the house. By then, it must have been late afternoon. The dinner dishes were all washed, and I'd finished paring and chopping the vegetables for supper.

I could almost hear Cook say, "No time for resting, Cinders! Step lively. In a kitchen there's always work to be done."

I remember straightening my aching back and thinking how weary I felt—tired enough, in truth, to die. I could not think of myself, though. Octavius alone mattered.

The clamor out front caught my ear then, and raised voices, one of which sounded like Markka's. But Markka had taken the children up to the garret for their naps.

Fear, trepidation, and curiosity made me tiptoe to the kitchen door and push it open. The voices came clearer: Markka and Mrs. Flick arguing.

"You must let them in."

"I must do nothing of the kind."

"They are permitted by King Edmund to see every woman of the town, should they request it. They have requested!"

"Get back to your work, stupid girl."

I crept down the hallway but a few steps. Now I could see them standing face to face in front of the closed front door.

"Let them in or I will report you to the authorities."

As might be expected, Mrs. Flick promptly struck out. Markka fell to the floor with a cry.

Mrs. Flick turned and saw me then. "You, drudge, back to the kitchen."

Drudge? Me? Once, yes, I had been. Once I was the girl who worked among the ashes, too ugly to lift her eyes and look anyone in the face.

Now I was—servant, yes. Mother to a Prince. Beloved of Rupert.

Beloved.

That thought gave me back the courage I seemed to have left beyond the walls of my kitchen prison. Instead of retreating back to the ashes, I went forward and, walking like a woman in a dream, pushed past Mrs. Flick.

Accompanied by her protests and abuse, I hauled open the door.

Too late. The men had already turned away. Two of them, yes, but I saw only their backs—one taller than the other, one aged, with whitened hair. They wore decent, ordinary clothes and…

Hearing the door open, the shorter of the two turned around.

My gaze fell first on the battered shoe in his hands. No crystal slipper, no, but one that had been worn much, scorched among the cinders, and nearly rubbed through. One stained by the dirt of the tunnel and molded to the shape of my foot.

I will remember until I die the moment I raised my eyes to his face. How long had it been? He looked as old and over-thin and worn as the object in his hands. Such an ordinary face to contain my world, all save those bright green eyes, one marked by a livid scar.

I squealed like a creature gone mad—barely a human sound—and threw myself into his arms. For an instant nothing else existed, not the past or future, not even Octavius, for whom I'd suffered so much—just the sensation of belonging that flowed between us and his arms clutching me tight. I might have stayed so forever, but Rupert at least remembered our son.

Into my ear he said, "Octavius?"

I drew away just far enough to look at him again. *Real. Here.* I smiled. "He's safe. Upstairs sleeping."

"My Queen," said the second man, and I turned to look at him in astonishment. Rellison—with tears in his eyes. "I am gratified beyond expression to see you."

Behind me, Mrs. Flick cleared her throat. Craning my neck, unwilling to let go of my husband, I saw she and Markka stood side by side in the doorway, Mrs. Flick staring, Markka with her face alight.

"Who do you think you are?" Mrs. Flick demanded of Rupert. "Unhand that girl. She is my servant."

Rupert drew himself up before giving a precise

bow. "I am Rupert, King of Burgendy. And, my good woman, you are mistaken. This is my wife, the Queen."

I will not say Mrs. Flick's expression was worth all I'd suffered, but it did come close.

Chapter Thirty

Hours later, when some of the excitement died down, once Rupert had been reunited with Octavius and Robin and we'd retired to the guest chamber in King Edmund's palace, he and I at last had a chance to speak together.

Rupert had a thousand questions, as did I. In all that time we'd thrown them at one another blindly, without opportunity to answer. Also in all that while, he'd barely let go of me or I of him, performing what tasks were needed with fused hands.

Not till nightfall did we stand looking at Octavius asleep in a clean cot, the world at last slowing enough for us to catch up.

"What happened in Burgendy?" I asked. "I confess, I feared you all dead."

Rupert blew out a breath. "A long and complicated tale. Suffice it to say, for now, we were able to refortify the wall and fight on." He shook his head in wonder. "Never let it be said the citizens of Burgendy are not fierce when attacked in their own nest. Right wasps they were. I have seen sights you would not believe—women repelling armed invaders using rolling pins and hat pins. Citizens battling in the very passageways where I played as a boy. Beating Ortis's men back by sheer force of will, so it seemed." He looked grim. "There were casualties. But the weather once more came to our aid."

His eyes met mine. "The turning point, though, was the death of Ortis."

"He is dead? How?"

"Once the wall fell, after I sent you away, he came storming in as if he thought he'd already won. A more cautious man might have held back till the victory had been secured, but who can blame him? He knew most of our men were wounded or slain and did not expect such resistance from our women."

He paused to kiss me. "Our women are beyond compare."

Much as I wanted to go on kissing him, I protested. "But…"

"Ortis came to me and demanded—once again—I surrender. A bad moment and no mistake. I did not know if I'd ever see you or Octavius again. I knew whatever terms of surrender he offered would be harsh. I decided to fight to the death and took him on."

"You killed him? In hand-to-hand battle?" My heart swelled.

Rupert's lips twisted. "I wish I could claim so. We were battling with the press of bodies all around us, and he fell from the wall—tumbled backward off the rubble he had, himself, created.

"It was not much of a fall—I did not believe him dead. I had other opponents, the fighting being very intense, but I saw his men pick him up and carry him away. We went back to defending, repelled the invaders, and closed the breach in the wall using pieces of the broken stone, furniture, anything to hand."

Rupert drew another breath, this one painful, and his fingers squeezed mine. "I went looking for you then, descended to the level where the tunnel opens. Mother told me you, Markka, and the children had gone on ahead. I tried to trace your course, but the tunnel had collapsed."

"Collapsed?"

He looked at me with agony in his eyes. "I feared the worst, thought I'd sent you to your death and our son with you. My love, I descended to the depths of despair. I no longer cared if I lived or died. But I had still a kingdom to defend."

"If you successfully repelled them then, why did it take you so long to come to Khett?"

"We did not repel them—at least, they did not withdraw, which made me believe Ortis to be still alive and directing maneuvers. For all I know he was still alive, if badly injured. They kept up the siege, though not so intense as it had been, until the weather broke.

"I will confess, then I feared the worst. We were out of fuel for the fires, out of food—out of hope. That's when the message came."

"Message?"

"From one of Ortis's generals. He said King Ortis was dead and his army would withdraw. He presented terms of peace."

Peace. It had seemed unreachable for so long.

Rupert drew me, by the hand, away from Octavius's cot to the edge of the bed.

"That's when the best part of the story comes. Cindra, my Cindra…" He caught my face between gentle hands and gazed into my eyes. "The truly amazing part. You must understand I believed the tunnel collapsed and you dead. Despite the peace, I could barely imagine going on.

"You must also know our people were equally devastated without you. They wept—spoke of your kindness, your compassion. Your beauty."

"Beauty?"

"Yes, love. They saw what I always saw in you—your spirit, shining."

"All except my mother."

"Darling, your mother is dead, as is your sister, Bethessa. They both fell in the fighting, after conducting themselves bravely."

"Bethessa, dead! And…you did not execute Mother as sentenced?"

"I did not have the chance."

I struggled to comprehend it; all the pain, cruelty, and yearning, gone.

"But I have not shared with you the best part of the story. In the midst of my despair, Mother came to me. She told me she'd spoken with Father's ghost. He bade me go search the tunnel again."

Rupert's eyes once more filled with tears.

He swallowed convulsively before he went on. "This time I took shovels and two of the lads but half grown. We excavated one of the branches and found only a sealed wall. We went back and took the right-hand passage, dug through the collapse I'd first found, and pressed on. It was close inside, and airless. I kept expecting to find your corpses."

"Oh, my love."

"Instead, after clearing two more falls, I found this." He picked up the battered slipper from the table beside the bed. "It was caught in a pile of dirt and rubble. I knew it for yours."

"The spot where I got stuck and fought my way

free."

"Beyond that place, the tunnel lay clear to the end. I could see the steps you fashioned in order to climb out. My brave and clever Queen."

He kissed me, a mark of devotion.

"But, Cindra, why did you not turn to King Edmund for help?"

"I did not know if I could trust him. I feared he might see Burgendy's downfall as an opportunity to seize control of Octavius and thus secure your kingdom for himself." I swallowed hard. "I might risk my safety…never his."

"Brave girl." Again he drew me to him; again I felt the hurt and fear drain from me.

"But you are wrong," he said in my ear.

"I am?"

"Yes, Cindra darling. You called Burgendy my kingdom. It is ours. Yours as well as Octavius's and mine. Did I not just tell you how the people love you? When I left to come searching, each one I met stopped me and begged, 'Bring her home, sire—bring her home.' "

I drew a breath that felt like my first in many days. "What now, Rupert?"

"We heal. We go home as the people have demanded and pick up the pieces, find our lost, if we can, and bury our dead. It will not be easy, but you, my love, are a healer by nature. I believe hard work and compassion will get us through."

"And," I smiled, "the advice of both your parents."

"Yes, my beautiful Queen."

Epilog

So you see, those who tell the tale did get some of it right. There was a wicked woman who had poisoned two of her daughters with selfishness and hate. There was a found slipper, though it was a battered, if cherished, specimen. No grand balls, though, and no magical coaches. But I do believe there was a fairy godmother who went—and still goes today—by the name of Markka.

All this, of course, happened many and many a year ago. Rupert, Octavius, and I did indeed return home to Burgendy. Everyone worked very hard to rebuild, recover our captured soldiers from Cardonay, and learn the fates of our dead, including my father who, I was told, perished fighting bravely somewhere north of the city. When possible, we collected their remains and provided honored burials. You may wonder what happened to my surviving sister, Nelissa; we had word from Cardonay, much later, that she'd fled the castle after the north wall fell and run off with one of Ortis's last remaining mercenaries. I never saw her again.

Eventually we succeeded in restoring the kingdom, but it became a far different place—much more humble, more of a community. Perforce, people had to help one another. Such tragedy as we'd faced could not be survived alone. Kindness thrived.

Rupert has always tried to give me credit for that. Undeserved, I'm sure—life teaches lessons, and the kingdom of Burgendy had been presented with a hard one. But I could not deny the remaining citizens, battered and worn as that old slipper of mine, were glad to see me. And I did my best to live up to the gift of their acceptance every day of my life.

Rupert and I are aged now. The Dowager Queen, the beloved mother for whom I'd always ached, has long gone from us. Octavius, who grew into a thoughtful man and married Dinnie, is now King, with Robin his trusted advisor. We have grandchildren.

Sometimes I tell them the story just as I have told it to you. For I think it should never be forgotten that the slippers—or indeed the bodies—we wear are nothing more than garments that drop away in time.

All the beauty lies beneath, and within. And how lucky am I that my Prince saw only that beauty when first he looked at me?

A word about the author…

Multi-award-winning author Laura Strickland delights in time traveling to the past and searching out settings for her books, be they Historical Romance, Steampunk, or something in between.

Born and raised in Western New York, she's pursued lifelong interests in lore, legend, magic, and music, all reflected in her writing. Although she enjoys travel, she's usually happiest at home, not far from Lake Ontario, with her husband and her "fur" child, a rescue dog.

Author of numerous Historical and Contemporary Romances, she is the creator of the Buffalo Steampunk Adventure series set in her native city.

www.ingramcontent.com/pod-product-compliance
Lightning Source LLC
Chambersburg PA
CBHW060925180626
46817CB00004B/1403

* 9 7 8 1 5 0 9 2 2 1 6 5 3 *